Under the Mountain Stars

Christina Rhoads

Under the Mountain Stars
Copyright © 2018 Christina Rhoads

ISBN: (ebook): 978-1-945910-54-8
(print): 978-1-945910-90-6

Inkspell Publishing
5764 Woodbine Ave.
Pinckney, MI 48169

Edited By Shelly Small

Cover art By Najla Qamber

DEDICATION

For the AW girls, without you this would not have happened

CHAPTER ONE

The truck and horse trailer veered towards the sickening drop-off beside the highway. Lenora pumped the brake pedal hard and checked her side-view mirror... sure enough, a blown trailer tire. With her heart hammering in her chest and a cold coil of fear in her stomach, she slowed the truck and horse trailer further and eased onto the highway shoulder. Turning on the hazard lights, she stepped out into the sharp wind and walked back to assess the damage. The tire was flat and beginning to shred. The thin mountain air and the reality of her predicament made her feel lightheaded.

She took three deep breaths. A flat tire is really nothing more than a good challenge, she tried to remind herself.

Opening the trailer door, she was greeted by a low nicker. Major, her Arabian horse, was eating hay, his dark eyes large with concern.

"We have a flat tire, my boy. I guess I better see if I can change this darn thing," Lenora said.

The realization that she was all alone on a mountain highway, thousands of miles from her old home, with her horse and a flat tire was really setting in. She took three more breaths and twisted her chestnut hair into a quick braid. After rummaging around in her emergency road kit, she found the right size socket for the trailer lug nut and a long breaker bar. Thankfully, she had a trailer jack. She set it in front of the good tire, then got back into her truck and slowly pulled the trailer forward. Only then did she remember that the lug nuts on the tire had to be loosened first. Choking back a laugh and then the tears stinging her eyelids, she backed the trailer off the jack. She then loosened the lug nuts, pulled the trailer back on the jack and removed the tire. Her spare was ready. She managed to lift it onto the exposed bolts and began the process of tightening the nuts. She wiped a stray curl out of her eyes with the back of one hand.

Fifteen minutes later she was leaning against the trailer with four good tires. She tried to wipe her hands off on some damp grass along the road. The action seemed pointless but made her feel like she was somewhat cleaner. She then stepped back into the horse trailer to check on Major one more time. Burying her face in his white mane, she let a couple of breathy sobs escape her wind-chapped lips before straightening up; it was time to drive again.

Lenora thought herself lucky to have had the flat tire before the sun disappeared behind the distant mountains. A contented smile crept to the corners of her lips. She did feel pretty proud of herself for changing the flat.

The mountain highway was steadily climbing, and the truck downshifted once again. To her left a huge vista opened up, and her heart soared; this was her grand adventure, one she knew she desperately needed. It had taken nearly a year of watching the last of her life fall to pieces around her to come to such a realization. Her marriage had ended, and her mother's death had become reality, before she accepted her aunt and uncle's offer to move to their ranch in the mountains.

Two hours outside of Missoula, Lenora saw the sign for the ranch up ahead and turned on the blinker. The dirt road was a rich red color. She looked through the pines but could not see a building, just fence stretching away into hills. Her heart began to sing. Something here felt good, yet oh-so-wild. A river edged the meadow full of sagebrush to the southeast, and the mountains reached down to cradle the land on three sides, creating a bowl full of meadows and hills. She found herself pressing the accelerator with vigor, making truck and trailer bounce along the rutted road. A mix of wonder, excitement, and anticipation stirred her stomach in a way that she had not experienced in a very long time.

As the truck crested a rise, Lenora saw the ranch spread out before her. The barn roofs looked as if they needed replacing. The place was not huge, but she found herself in love with it already. It was a little smaller than she remembered from her one visit as a child but just as beautiful. The truck eased down the slope to the ranch and then up the rise to the barns. Lenora turned off the engine and climbed out feeling stiff and suddenly very tired. The door to the ranch house swung open, and two dogs followed her aunt out onto the big spread of porch. Aunt Annie's copper hair caught the setting sun to the west, and her smile instantly welcomed Lenora.

"You made it! How was the drive? I wish you would have just had that horse shipped. But I understand of course," Annie said in one breath. "I've just worried so much about you driving alone. All those long, long miles and all."

She opened her arms and hugged Lenora. The thin air, the long drive, feeling safe for the first time since her mother's death; suddenly tears were a blink away. The dogs stood around wagging their tails. Annie let Lenora go but kept her hand resting on her niece's shoulder.

Lenora looked around at the simple, log ranch house and the large barns. There was a corral to Lenora's left, and she could see cattle to the west grazing in the setting sun. Beyond the cows were mountains and hills, huge rolling slopes followed by steep peaks. The sheer beauty of the place seemed overwhelming to Lenora. From the corner of her eye, she could see her aunt watching her.

"What do you think?" Annie asked.

"It's beautiful," Lenora replied.

"Hey! You made it," Uncle Byron called, as he appeared around the side of one of the barns.

He was a tall man with wide shoulders and a bit of stomach. His gray mustache would have looked ridiculous back in Chicago, but seemed perfect paired with the ranch and setting sun. He smiled and reached out to grasp Lenora's other shoulder.

"Welcome to Bear Dance Ranch. We're so glad you're here. We really are," he said. "Now, let's get this fancy horse of yours unloaded. What did you say he is, an Arabian?"

Lenora nodded.

"Hmm, well I guess we better have a look at him," Byron said.

Lenora unlatched the trailer clasp, and her uncle opened the back door of the horse trailer. Major stepped out and snorted as he arched his beautiful neck. His glossy coat caught the dying sun and he tossed his head. Lenora could not help but smile, Major was always one to show off.

"Well, he sure is something," Her uncle said.

"He's a good-looking animal. Nice conformation, and heart, it looks like, too," said a man's voice coming from just behind the small group.

Lenora turned and found herself staring at the man. She politely looked down as she felt her neck and cheeks heat with embarrassment.

"Lenora, this is Clay Darkhorse," Annie said with a smile. "He's the ranch foreman your uncle told you about. He's helped us here at the ranch for a long time now. He's also quite the horse trainer, you know."

Lenora did remember her uncle saying something about a ranch foreman, or a "right-hand man," as he put it, but for some reason she had pictured an aging white man sitting around talking about the good old days with her aunt and uncle. Instead, the man that stood in front of her was dark-skinned, dressed in snug, worn jeans with a little mud in his black hair and eyes that made her feel like she was standing in front of him in lingerie. Man, those eyes, she thought.

She knew she had better not look directly at him. A little late, she realized he was talking to her.

"I hope the drive was good," he said, looking expectantly at her with a half-smile slowly appearing on his lips.

The top button was undone on Clay's shirt, and she could just make out the definition of his chest, beautifully shaped by years of ranch work, she imagined. He stood with a relaxed grace, his hands open and palms facing towards her. She wondered if he was Lakota, perhaps from a local tribe. She wanted to ask but instead opted to answer his question.

"Yes. Fine. Really long though," Lenora said. "I had a flat on Ninety-three, but I got it changed okay."

She held up her still-blackened hands from the tire as evidence. At that moment, her hair took full advantage of an opportunity to make a dramatic appearance and broke loose of the rubber band that had previously held it captive, falling around her face and halfway down her back.

She could think of nothing else to say except 'you're gorgeous' so she remained quiet, trying her best to smooth her hair away from her face with her less-than-clean hands. She could only imagine what she must look like after her long drive and tire-changing episode.

"What? A flat tire? I told you she shouldn't have driven all that way," Annie scolded.

Lenora was not sure if her aunt was talking to her or her uncle.

"It's okay, really! I changed it and still made it to the ranch before dark." Lenora tried to reassure her aunt.

Annie was glaring at Byron. There was an awkward pause.

"Can I get him settled for you?" Clay asked, nodding towards Major.

Was she imagining it, or was he staring at her? She hoped she had not rubbed black dirt onto her face in her attempts to control her own wild mane.

"So, did you change the tire yourself?" Clay asked.

"Yeah. My horse didn't want to help," Lenora said. She felt stupid as soon as the words left her mouth. She chided herself silently for always having a snarky reply.

"Good job." Clay grinned. He let Major sniff his hands before taking the lead rope and walking her horse towards the barn.

"I hate to leave him in a new place, can I come?" Lenora felt her cheeks burn again but did not even know why.

"Yes, of course." Clay was smiling. "You can go in and get settled, and then I'll come get you. I'll show you where your horse is staying, and maybe give you a quick tour of the ranch."

"Good idea, Clay," Annie said.

And with that, Clay led Major towards the barn, and Annie, Byron, and Lenora made their way to the house.

The front steps were huge, hand-hewn timbers and the wrap around porch reminded her of the house from *Legends of the Fall* with its weathered, part-of-the-land feel. The front door led to a large entry with two benches and shelves for boots. A large assortment of coats and jackets for every season hung along the wall. Beyond the entry, a dining room and kitchen merged into one open area with a large fireplace surrounded by heavy chairs and a table. Annie showed Lenora a seemingly new Viking stove and large white farm style sink. Two long windows opened up above a long counter and cutting board, shedding light into the kitchen and giving a breathtaking view of the river fringing the meadows.

"Are you cooking again?" Annie asked.

"How about breakfast in the morning?" Lenora replied.

She felt her body relax as the words left her mouth. Cooking in the mountains sounded just right, she thought.

She would find a new way forward, and it would be good, maybe even wonderful, after some time of course, but for now *good* would be just fine for her she decided.

Annie led her up the staircase, which was almost as solid as the outside porch. At the top of the landing several doors lined the hallway. Annie led Lenora to the last door, which opened into a large room with both south- and west-facing windows.

"It has a private bath," Annie said. "I hope it's okay?"

Her aunt seemed unsure, and so Lenora smiled and touched the other woman's shoulder. "It's perfect."

Lenora walked to the window and gazed out at the last of the sunset. The colors were purple and gray, and the shadows were long. She brushed her fingers across the window frame and felt a deep hollowness. She turned back into the room and saw her aunt watching her.

"How are you holding up?" Annie asked.

"I think better. I'm glad I came. Sometimes, at moments like this, I..." Lenora looked away as a lump made its presence known in her throat, "I find myself thinking about calling her. And telling her about my day. All about my adventures."

"I'm sorry. I'm so glad you came though. I can't imagine you all alone in that horrible city. This is your home now, if you want it to be."

"Thanks, Aunt Annie," Lenora said.

Byron came through the doorway with two of Lenora's bags and behind him was a thin guy in his late teens.

"This is Jesse," Byron said.

The young man smiled shyly at Lenora through his shaggy forelock.

"Get settled in. And then come down. Clay will show you around the place," Annie said.

Lenora unpacked some of her clothes but realized she was far too tired to try and face sorting through what was left of her old life. Her uncle and Jesse brought up the last of her things. It was funny how she had managed to dwindle her belongings down to a suitcase and a few bags. She laid out a picture of her mother. It had been taken on one of the last fun days they had enjoyed, before the chemo had drained all the vitality from her mother. In the picture, they pressed their cheeks together and posed like best friends for a selfie on Lenora's phone. She gave the picture a quick kiss before pulling on her jacket.

Out on the porch, the shadows were gray and the light of dusk haunting. She made her way out into the yard and found Clay in the first barn. A dog rubbed against his leg and he stroked its ears as Lenora approached.

"This is Suzie. She's a good herding dog, but an even better companion," Clay said. Another dog appeared behind Lenora and sniffed her pant leg in a friendly way.

"That's Sam," Clay said. He motioned to the dog who was introducing himself to Lenora.

She touched Sam's velvet ears with her fingertips and then knelt and stroked his black and white face.

Clay gave Suzie one more pat, nodded to Lenora, and led the way into the barn. Major was eating hay and looked relaxed. He nuzzled Lenora's hand but then went back to his food.

"He looks happy. Thanks for getting him situated," Lenora said.

"Sure. I'll show you the rest of the barns. And then, if you feel up to it, I'll take you out to see some of the pastures. Tomorrow, though," Clay said.

"That would be great," she said, her heart picking up speed.

She wondered if Clay was part of her aunt and uncle's plan to cheer her up. Surely not. They must need a lot of help on the ranch, and they probably did not want her flirting with the foreman. Also, she got the idea that Clay was more than just an employee to them, maybe like the son they had never had. She knew she had better be careful; her heart could not take any more jostling.

She wished she knew how to properly ask what tribe he was from. After living in the city most of her life, she had little experience with Native Americans. She felt awkward; like a rude, white person. No one ever asked from which European country she originated.

Clay showed her the outdoor pens and several barns. There were pastures with young horses and lots of cows with calves.

"In a month or so we'll take all these momma cows, as well as their new calves, up to the summer pasture," Clay said. "We run around one hundred and fifty head of cattle this time of year."

Lenora had never been around cows. Back east she had worked at a local barn and trained quite a few horses, but this was a whole new world to her. They continued on their tour and stopped next to a long, high-roofed building.

"I'd really like to turn this into an indoor arena. I need a place to train horses in the winter when the weather is bad," Clay said.

He glanced at her and then looked away quickly. His dark eyebrows framed the most beautiful long-lashed eyes she had ever seen on a man.

"We had better get you inside for dinner," Clay said.

Lenora realized that she must look tired. Thankfully, he would never know how bad she had looked a month ago. She saw herself vividly, cleaning stalls at the horse barn where Major had been boarded, her unwashed hair knotted in a bun and eyes ringed by dark shadows; sleeping had become more than difficult after her mother's death. That was in the past, she reminded herself. Today she was touring her new home with a surprisingly handsome guide.

Inside the ranch house a fire was burning in the hearth and the smell of beef stew and cornbread filled the kitchen. Lenora tried to help carry out plates and silverware, but was shooed out of the kitchen by her aunt and uncle. She picked a chair at the large table with a view of the glowing fire and drank the glass of red wine Jesse handed her. Once everyone was seated and food had been passed around, conversation ran to cattle, fence, and pastures. Lenora listened, feeling a little overwhelmed. There was no doubt in her mind she was a good hand with horses, but this whole ranch business was new to her and a lot to take in. She wondered if she would fit in with this close-knit group of people whom she barely knew. She tried to remind herself they were her family.

"The River Meadow will need worked on. I saw at least

two places where whole sections of fence have been washed away with the floods from melted snow," Clay said.

"Jesse, you'd better get started on that in the morning," Byron said.

"How are those two new mares coming along, Clay?" Annie asked.

"Good. Both are loping well and ready to go out on the range. They haven't bucked once with me this whole week," Clay said.

"Clay takes in outside horses for training to help keep this place going," Annie said.

Lenora nodded because her mouth was full. They were a big family she realized. After being seldom in human company during her long drive west, and even before that, as the shambles of her marriage came to a shuddering halt, she was unused to conversation. Her head felt thick and her mind blank. There would be a great deal to learn starting tomorrow. Hopefully, sleep would help her mind regain some of its quickness. Maybe she would find joy in the company of others, or at least she hoped so.

The feeling of loneliness caught her off guard as she climbed the stairs to her new room after dinner. She told herself this was a new beginning, and no matter what it had to be better than the hell she was leaving behind; an empty life without her mother, a failed job and an ex-husband who already had a serious new girlfriend.

Walking to the windows in her room, she opened one of them. Outside, the air was crisp and alive. She took a deep breath and found herself imagining riding out through the purple hills and into the mountains beyond. She could smell sage grass, cows and maybe a hint of wood smoke. There was something magical about this place, alive with the promise of a fresh start. Deep inside, she was holding an empty place, waiting for life to fill it with new adventures and gifts.

CHAPTER TWO

Mornings were going to be special at the ranch, she realized as soon as she woke to mist shrouding the mountains to the north. Downstairs, the coffee pot filled the large kitchen with the smell of morning. The dogs were underfoot, and everyone looked happy even though their faces were still puffy from sleep. She asked Clay and her uncle to give her some chores and they obliged: feeding and turnout of the ranch and training horses. After her chores she promised everyone breakfast and found herself enjoying the rich, easterly light as she made egg and biscuit sandwiches. The ranch kitchen was big and comfortable, and her aunt was happy to concentrate on accounts at her desk while Lenora took over breakfast. Lenora mixed the biscuit dough from scratch, and then rolled and placed neatly shaped rounds on a well-oiled cooking sheet. While the biscuits baked, she searched for preserves to top them and discovered a jar of apple butter in the refrigerator.

When the men came in they were hungry and smelled of the morning chores: mud, horses, alfalfa, and wood shavings. Lenora felt her nostrils flare with the smells of life on the ranch.

"So, are you going to cook for us every morning,

Lenora?" Byron asked.

"Maybe," Lenora replied, "Do you want me to?"

"Yes!" Both Jesse and Clay replied simultaneously.

Lenora smiled and felt warmth fill her. Maybe she could belong here.

Annie came into the kitchen and smiled to see the men eating blissfully around the table and Lenora cooking.

As everyone rinsed their plates and put them in the dishwasher, Clay paused next to Lenora.

"Would you like to have a riding tour of the ranch? Maybe this afternoon?" He asked.

"Yes. Yes, I would," Lenora said.

She found herself staring up at his dark eyes and feeling lightheaded.

She knew now was not the time to start falling for the first cowboy she met. Especially not one who was such an important part of her aunt and uncle's ranch.

She took a deep breath as he walked out of the kitchen. She could not help but notice the snug fit of his jeans. She concluded that riding horses must really be good for a man's backside.

After lunch Lenora unpacked her bags and all her tack from the horse trailer. Then she met Clay in the corral. He caught a big sorrel mare and a paint gelding.

"I thought you might ride a ranch horse today. That way your boy can have some time to get used to the place and recover from the long trip," Clay said.

"Good idea," Lenora responded.

They brushed and saddled Moon, the mare, and Big Sky, the gelding, in easy silence.

It was not until they were through the ranch gate that Clay spoke. "I'm glad you've come. It will be so good for Annie to have you around. You know she's wanted you and your mom here for so long?"

Lenora was quiet for a long moment. "I actually didn't know that," she finally answered. "I don't know exactly why Mom didn't want to come here very much. But I wish that I would have come more, even if it was on my own."

Clay did not elaborate further and they continued in silence through the open pasture land. She looked at the mountains to the east. They rode gradually up and away from the ranch, along a winding two-track road paved with loose rock and grass. On each side of the road were aspen and pine trees. Further up she thought she saw a grove of spruce, but realized she would need to look through her plant and tree books to learn more about the flora and fauna of her new home.

"Sometimes, a person has to get away from where they started," Clay said.

Lenora was shaken from her reverie of the trees and reminded of her mother who had been born on the plains just east of Missoula. She had left Montana at eighteen years old and returned only three times. Annie, her mother's older sister, had stayed and married a rancher and moved up into the mountains. Despite being her mother's older sister, Annie was a woman whom Lenora knew very little about. She had never known much about any of her family out west, she realized. Her mother had never told Lenora a great deal about her father. The basic story Lenora knew was that her mother had been young and become pregnant by a cowboy. According to her mother, the man was hardly ready to be a father; and so the decision was obvious— as simple as packing her bags and boarding a train. Lenora had always had the impression that her mother never looked back. Now Lenora was trying to discover a world her mother had not shared with her.

"I suppose they do," she said in reply to Clay's earlier statement.

Big Sky was solid and sure-footed under Lenora, who found herself wanting a good canter to clear her mind. She turned to Clay and found him watching her. She smiled, surprised to find his eyes on her.

"Can we canter?" She asked.

As an answer he grinned; a lopsided smile, and gestured

her first.

She kissed to her horse and felt him gather his haunches and then leap into a full-shouldered lope. The mountain wind was cool and fresh against her face. She felt the thin air moving through the horse's lungs as he surged beneath her. She took a deep gulp herself. The track narrowed ahead, and she urged her horse onward and upwards. It was not until they reached a plateau where she could see the whole bowl of the valley stretching below that she let her horse ease back into a walk. She turned and surveyed the land beneath and felt a pulse of pure joy; a kind she had not felt in a long time, shoot through her body. This was an adventure! She knew she needed adventure in her life. More importantly, she needed the promise that there was more living yet to be done. For too long she had felt as if her life was over, each chapter kept closing in such a painful way.

She turned back to her silent guide and found him surveying the valley as well, a smile lighting his face.

"It's so nice to come up here," Clay said. "To see the world from above always helps me remember my place in it."

Lenora looked at him and smiled in agreement. Her hair was free again and blowing in the wind.

His words rang true. She could be happy up here because her troubles seemed small and contained to the human size. While on the mountain, the whole world was huge and simply gorgeous with its massive layout. It was good to see her life from this perspective she realized, to know her worries and fears were proportionately small in the grand scheme of things.

Life at the ranch began to take on a tentative shape. Lenora found herself immersed in the spring awakening of her new world in the mountains. Clay seemed happy to let her into his routine. She watched him prepare the ranch horses for work, and, slowly, he began to let her help. It was a learning process for both of them, she soon realized. Her way of handling horses and dealing with the sticky situations that arose when working with these large, opinionated animals was different than his. He dropped the long ropes on the ground as he taught the colts how to steer. She, on the other hand, found herself compulsively keeping her lines tidy and the horses well groomed. Climbing onto a youngster, Clay would laugh if they bucked and plunged. While Lenora lunged and prepped each of her horses meticulously in order to avoid any unforeseen bronco moments. She thought she saw him laughing at her as she obsessively cleaned the horses' saddles and bridles. Who cares what he thinks, she reminded herself.

When the day was fresh she would perch on the top rail of the corral and watch him with a young horse. His body would remain loose and relaxed and his face intent, until he would turn towards her and flash a quick smile to acknowledge her presence, at which point she found her heart leaping just like the young horses. She would smile back, how could she not? There was something boyish about him despite the starting of crow's feet around his eyes and his well-muscled manliness.

As she helped Clay saddle up a horse, their hands would sometimes brush. She found herself looking forward to these stolen moments when they stood so close together.

That night in bed she let herself imagine turning into his touch. She let her mind trace the outline of his chest, the lean shape of his torso hardened by ranch work.

She jerked herself back to reality and lay still in her bed. She needed to heal, she reminded herself, not fall headlong into the arms of a cowboy. Outside her window the sky was rich with stars. She slipped out from under the covers and opened the window. The air was not warm exactly, but it didn't have the teeth of winter she had felt every night since her arrival.

She dressed quietly in jeans, a thick flannel shirt, and a jacket. She found her boots in the dark entryway and managed to put them on while at the same time petting the dogs to keep them quiet. They raised their heads and thumped their tails against the rugs her aunt laid out for them. Only Sam wanted to come out into the starlit night with her. She was grateful for the company and stepped into the magic of a spring mountain night. The air caressed her cheeks with a nip of chill making her glad for her flannel, while also carrying the scent of growing things. She made her way to the pasture where Major spent his nights and climbed over the fence. The outlines of the hills were dark against the fullness of the sky. The horses had heard her, and came over to investigate. Major, realizing it was his human making the night visit, pinned his ears at the others horses and kept Lenora to himself. She stroked his neck and hunted in her pockets for something to feed him, eventually producing a somewhat shriveled bit of carrot. Major took it appreciatively and did not seem the least offended that it was far from fresh. Lenora rested her forehead against his shoulder as he nibbled on spring grass. She remembered her mother singing a lovely French song. *How had it gone?*

"...sous les etoiles de montagne," she hummed and then let a few notes fill the still air. Major raised his head, and Sam wagged his tail. She realized she was not alone a moment before a tall shadow separated from the general darkness. Lenora sucked in her breath while sternly ordering herself to be calm. Neither the dog nor horse was upset, so this must be someone from the ranch whom they knew, she told herself.

"I thought it might be you. Out on a night like this."

Lenora felt herself flush. It was almost as if she had conjured Clay from the very darkness of her overactive imagination. Careful with those fantasies, she cautioned herself.

"Yes, well. It seemed as if the air had lost some of the winter feel. And I couldn't sleep," she said. She purposefully kept her tone light.

"Me neither."

Lenora laced her fingers through Major's mane and looked at the shadow that was Clay.

"Can you ride him bareback?" Clay asked.

"Yes, of course," Lenora replied.

"Wanna go up into the hills? Just a little?" His voice was definitely intimate as he stepped towards her.

"Yes."

She had not thought about her answer before the quick reply left her lips. It was so true though, she wanted nothing more than to just ride into the secret, starry night with this man.

He gentled one of the mares turned out in Major's pasture and slipped a halter over her head. He came over to Lenora who led her own horse to the corral gate and used it to mount. She saw a flash of white teeth in the dark and then watched him vault onto his mare's back. He landed so gently upon the horse she barely flicked an ear. Then he opened the gate from horseback and they were loose in the night.

"Show off," Lenora said.

She heard him laugh and saw a flash of teeth again.

The sky was a blanket of thick darkness, rich in its depth and heavy with stars so bright they lit the earth below. Lenora breathed in mountain air and felt a deep-seated knot between her shoulder blades release. She really had no idea she had even been carrying tension. Her life— her past life in Chicago— was slipping away one knot at a time. Breathing in a lungful of night air, she spoke silently to her mother. If only, Lenora thought, her mother could see the stars from the mountain tonight. Why did she have to leave and never come back to her home? Why had her mother not shared this world with her? Lenora did not understand what had kept her away, and somehow that made her mad when all she really wanted was to have her mother here, on this horse, under these stars.

Clay was slowing down, holding his mare back until they were riding knee to knee. She felt the brush of his leg against hers and imagined for a moment his hand caressing the length of her thigh. And just like that her mind came back from the past and her mother to settle in the present, glorious moment.

"What are you thinking about?" Clay asked.

Lenora felt her face and neck warm and was thankful starlight was not bright enough to reveal her red cheeks.

"The stars aren't so brilliant back home," she said instead of the truth.

"It's this mountain air. So thin and clear, it's almost like riding up into the sky. You know, the Lakota have many legends about the stars. The Milky Way…" Clay said and then paused.

He raised his arm and pointed up and slightly to the west at the thick mass of stars melding together. They almost appeared pure white in places.

"The Milky Way, *Wanaghi Tachanku*, which means trail of the spirits, is a trail that all people must take at the end, when fate overcomes them for the final time. Maybe she's there. Maybe your mother is now on the trail." He let his words fill the vast, living silence. He seemed to genuinely wish that she could find comfort in the wildness of the mountains.

Lenora watched him closely as he gazed up at the sky. She could feel her heart hammering in her chest. How had he known about her silent, cerebral invite of her mother on this midnight trail ride? She wondered if she could trust this man. He seemed real and true and solid, but was that actually so?

They rode further into the hills until the ranch was small behind them. Major was sure-footed in the dark and she smiled to herself, realizing how well he had adapted to this huge change in his life. He did not seem to miss his comfy stall and small pasture back in Illinois at all. She realized that she too would not go back at this point in time. Curiosity about the future here at Bear Dance Ranch and, if she was honest, about this man drew her steadily forward.

He stopped his mare at the crown of the next hill and she stopped Major next to him. He pointed up into the sky and she saw the Little Dipper, and then he pointed out the Hunter stalking its prey across the expanse of night, and she kind of saw it. She was so entranced by the clear air and feathery light she would not have been surprised to see the real huntsmen come forward from the shadows. She could swear there was magic in this place. Her Western Adventure had begun in earnest and she realized that her mother's passing had been a push for her to leave the Midwest and come here to find her roots and maybe even herself. She was deep in thought as the stars shone overhead. Their knees bumped, and she felt the familiar jolt of electricity and realized he was looking at her.

"You feel it too?" He said.

She was not sure what he meant: the jolt of attraction or the beauty of night; the clear stars so close they could almost be reached?

So she said, "The stars are magical. Aren't they?"

"Yes." He looked back up, and she could breathe again.

Slowly, they turned the horses back to the ranch and were quiet as they made their way home. She felt tired now and ready for her bed and time to recap in the privacy of her room about the crazy way Clay made her pulse surge. What was she doing? She really could not even believe that she was feeling anything at all. In an odd way, it made her happy that at least she felt something after such a long period of feeling as if she was simply a husk of a human. Maybe a little crazy attraction was okay.

Wrapped up in her own head and feeling a little drowsy she slipped off Major when they stopped at the pasture gate. Clay let her pass through first and she pulled the halter and rope off Major's head and let him go with a gentle pat of thanks for the lovely night ride. Clay let his mare go and then closed the gate behind them.

"Thanks for taking me up," she said. "It was really great."

"Sure, any night," he said.

They both hesitated for a moment, and then Lenora found herself hurrying towards the house and waving awkwardly goodbye. She knew she had just panicked but there was no fixing it now.

She pulled off her boots on the porch and tried not to let

the storm door bang behind her. She told the dogs to be quiet and left them on their rugs in the entryway and then made her way up to her bedroom.

She strongly doubted that this cowboy was really interested in her, anyway. She was probably making a big deal over him trying to be nice to her. She was sure he felt bad that her mother had died and she was having a hard time dealing with it. He most likely had a girlfriend in every town with a rodeo. This was the last guy in the world who would find her interesting. She imagined he would be into those rhinestone-studded, bleached blondes with lots of lipstick. She could not even remember the last time she had worn lipstick, and her hair was the color of the inside of a pecan shell. She was not a rhinestone beauty queen. She even rode an Arabian. What must this man think of her? She fell asleep with a smile on her lips. For the first time in too long she had a tingle of excitement below her ribcage about what the next morning would bring.

CHAPTER THREE

Her days began with chores: feeding horses, bringing in the orphaned calves that needed bottle fed, and cleaning stalls. After that there was making breakfast for her aunt, uncle, Jesse and Clay. Slowly, she had taken over the task of cooking for everyone and found herself enjoying the job a great deal. The simple pleasure she found standing in front of the stove and mixing ingredients surprised her, and began to give her life the sweet shape of routine. She worked on creating new recipes in the evenings, then in the mornings she put together ingredients lists and drove the twenty miles to the store. Her aunt was more than happy to give most of the kitchen duties to Lenora, though she still helped in the evenings. Lenora found herself enjoying the time spent with her aunt as the sun settled in the west, and they prepared dinner together.

One such evening, Annie was pulling scalloped potatoes out of the oven. It was Friday and the day had been especially cold and windy. Lenora had decided the men needed hearty food. She was grating beets to add to the salad when she found herself humming. Annie set the casserole dish on the counter to cool and turned to Lenora, enfolding her in her hay-scented sweater.

"It's good to see some color in your cheeks," Annie said.

Lenora looked up to see her aunt's eyes alive with the shine of unshed tears and realized how much she was starting to feel like herself.

"I think I like the mountains," Lenora replied.

She could not say anything else. She could not find the words to describe the late night ride into the starry hills with Clay, or the strawberry and orange sunrises when she woke. She could not explain how the walk to the corral with dew dampening her boots and the horses there to greet her with hungry nickers made her feel. There was fear that if she put into words the joy she felt creating a recipe for the new people in her life, somehow some of the magic would fade. She did not quite trust herself to speak of these things yet. If she tried to explain them and search for the words, she was scared that these basic joys would flee and leave her once again alone, with no way to move towards the new and stronger person she wished to become.

There, in fact, lay the whole core of the issue; she now wanted to grow stronger and find a way forward. Before her move west, she could not even imagine herself becoming something after her mother's death and the sudden end to her marriage. This, of course, embarrassed her; to confess she could not see herself without her mother or a husband, even if he was a rotten one. What kind of independent woman admitted this? Perhaps, in part it was because she and her mother had been so close; there had never been a father in her life to bridge the gap between the outside world and the one her mother had built for just the two of them. Perhaps she would have been the same either way. Perhaps she would have been empty and lost no matter her relationship with her paternal father. Regardless, she was here now; and she would grow slowly and let the pain be a little less every day.

The men came in and washed up at the sink as Lenora finished the beets. Her aunt set out stacks of dishes for the men to carry with them on their way to the table. Clay came up beside Lenora, smiling in what she almost thought was a shy way. She felt her palms grow sweaty and she hoped the warmth on her neck was not a flush. Was this man really flirting with her?

"Can I carry the salad out?" Clay asked, and before Lenora could respond he continued, "Are there beets in it?"

Lenora found herself looking up into his eyes and having a hard time forming an answer.

"Yes," she said, finally.

She was going crazy out here in the wilds. Just because the first man who had paid attention to her in a long while was cute, a cowboy, and sat a horse like he had been born on one, did not mean she had to go all soft in the head. She quickly looked away from his eyes and promised herself she would not go night riding with him anymore. Right, she thought.

After the hearty meal, her aunt supervised the cleanup. Lenora had been banned from the kitchen after dinner, and so she stepped out on the porch to write in her journal in the growing duskiness. The breeze in the pines next to the house was hypnotic and almost like waves on the beach. Taking a deep breath, she could taste the tang of sap from the awakening trees. She felt him approach, lifting her head as he sat next to her on the porch swing.

He did not look at her for a minute, and she let the silence lay between them without the disturbance of a ripple on its perfect surface.

"Do you want to ride with me up to Bear Peak tonight? The moon is almost full. And, well, the weather is perfect," Clay said. She imagined his voice sounded hopeful.

She let the question stand in front of them, quivering a little in the fading light. He was doing more than befriending her; she could feel the air between them textured with curiosity and, maybe, a strand of desire soft and wispy like the smell of honeysuckle in late June. She looked out into the night and imagined riding through the darkness, which would suddenly seem less dark as they left the artificial lights of the ranch and moved into the silent night of the mountains. The air would be soft and laced with the warming sap of red pines.

"Yes." The word felt seductive as it left her lips, and she could not help but glance at him. He was watching her and his eyes were shadowed. She thought she saw a glint of something that made her stomach tighten low down and a thrill like she had not felt in a long time run through her body.

"I'll saddle your horse if you want to go change? It might be a little colder up there." Clay laced his fingers together and looked at his hands.

"Thank you. Yeah, I'll go now," Lenora said.

She stood and he did as well, and they were suddenly very close. Lenora wished she could think of something funny to say but her mind was already galloping away on Major. She turned and went into the house, and, when she looked behind her, he had disappeared into the near darkness.

She put on a thick flannel and tights under her jeans, and then her jacket and a scarf for her neck. She was glad she did not encounter her aunt or uncle as she left the house and did not have to explain her night ride with the cowboy. Outside, the moon was just starting to rise, its shoulders hunched large on the horizon, and a jolt of pure joy shot through her so quickly that she was taken by surprise at its intensity. She was alive. She breathed in and out. It was wonderful to see life again as an adventure, and not this horrible thing to be constantly watched and feared and worried over.

He was waiting for her with Major and his mare, Moon, by the gate to the corral. She could not help but like the way he looked standing there with two horses, his head slightly bowed as he adjusted the stirrups on her saddle. Major stood close to him perfectly calm and she liked this too; how her horse was relaxed with this man, the way she had noticed that all horses were. The air smelled fresh, as if things were beginning to grow. She realized spring would give way to summer, and then who knew the crazy way she might feel?

He smiled at her and she saw his eyes were anything but tame— full of horses and the wildness of the mountains. She felt a tingle run through her thighs, making her want nothing more than to ride into the complete wildness of the dark night and leave behind any worry, fear or thought from the past. She would surrender to the night and this man, letting the darkness and peace of the mountains remake her in the process. She stepped up to the three of them her mind awakened by the cool spring air. Clay handed her Major's reins and held the horse's bridle while she mounted. Then he rested his hand very lightly on her thigh and looked up at her where she sat astride her horse. The starlight and the coolness of the moon bathed his face. She abruptly realized that this man saw her, really saw her. It was disconcerting, frightening even, and yet the most exhilarating rush of pleasure flowed through her body.

She could not explain how this stranger, from a different way of life and from a very different culture, could possibly know her, when she herself often felt confused by her own emotions, fears and mixed desires.

His voice was intimate when he spoke, and his hand still rested firm but light as bird wings on her thigh.

"I'm glad you want to come out with me. There's something special about riding at night," he said. "At least, I've always thought so."

She looked down at him, feeling warmth flood up from where his hand rested on her leg, and smiled as best she could.

"Yes. I feel it here," Lenora said. She touched her heart.

He mounted his mare, and they rode out of the ranch gate and into the great vastness of the mountains, lining the horizon with dark edges.

The trail wound up and up. They stopped twice to let the horses breathe; speaking quietly, as if the silence of the night should not be disturbed by human voices. He told her a little about his upbringing, which had occurred not too far from the mountains in which they now rode. She in turn told him some about her life before her mother had died. They talked of childhood and its mystery as it flees in front of adulthood. He sat loose and relaxed in the saddle, and she watched him when he rode in front of her. Major was well behaved, not shying at shadows like he often did. She thought the move out west had been good for him as well, forcing him to give up some of his spoiled habits of being spooky and temperamenta. She wondered if perhaps those habits had been from boredom and lack of exercise and perhaps even from lack of adventure. Horses needed adventure just like humans, and Major was an Arabian, a breed of horse known for their intelligence and bravery. This was the adventure they had both needed.

The trail was long and wound through pine forests and the silvery trunks of aspen. When they finally neared the top, the trees gave way to barren rock and loose sage mapped the ground beneath their horses' feet. The stars were so brilliant. Lenora felt her breath catch in her throat as the tail of a shooting star arced across the dark dome overhead, almost as if the night sky were saying hello to them as they reached the peak of the mountain. To be sure, this was not the tallest peak, but it did rise by itself, and, though it was low and less jagged than the others to the north and east, it had a quiet splendor about it. Lenora felt herself smiling as she imagined the mountain welcoming them to traverse its quiet sides in the peace of the night.

"What do you think?" Clay said.

"It's so beautiful." Lenora did not know what else to say.

"I thought you would like it. You know, not everyone appreciates the beauty of this place. The… the grandeur of it," Clay said.

"That's funny because that's how I pictured the mountain. You know? As grand somehow. Just like it's this special being or something," she trailed off feeling silly.

He laughed and she smiled a little.

He was looking at her, and she felt her stomach quiver. She could not read his face in the darkness, but she imagined, or maybe felt, some tingle of hot desire moving between the space separating their horses. What was she doing up on this mountain with the man who helped her aunt and uncle with everything they did at the ranch? Why must she automatically think that it would end badly, when it had not even started yet?

Then Clay was off his horse, letting the reins slip from his fingers, and she felt his hands on her waist. He was looking up at her, and the frantic swirl of thoughts and worries in her head stopped. Lenora felt shock going through her sides and mind. She realized he did want her.

He was pulling her off her horse, and she let him.

"I can't kiss you up there. And I can't wait any longer, with you staring at me with those huge doe-eyes," Clay said.

"Sorry," Lenora said.

"Don't ever be sorry for being you." His voice was low, his words meant for her ears alone.

She did not know what else to say, and she could not think straight with his hands on her waist. Once Lenora was secure on the ground, Clay bent his head towards hers and she could feel all the long leanness of him against her. Her mind was blank, and the stars and thin air were not helping. He was kissing her so gently she felt herself relax, but even this was deadly. She found her mouth opening and she wanted him to possess her. She pressed back against him and felt his tongue tease her tongue. He was gentle, letting her lead him. His fingers moved from her waist up her back, and he soon was tangled in her hair. He did not seem to want to stop, and she could not ever remember a first kiss that had lasted so long or was so deep. He pulled away and she could breathe, but he only wanted to kiss her neck and her jaw. His lips were fire, or maybe water, she felt herself losing ground under them, losing herself to this delight.

"You smell like jasmine," he whispered in her ear.

His tongue flicked across her collarbone, and she

31

wrapped her arms around his neck to keep her footing.

"Do you know what jasmine smells like?" She said.

Her voice sounded breathless to her own ears, but she was proud of herself for being able to speak coherently. He laughed and pulled back while still keeping his hands on her.

"No, not a clue. But, I imagine it would smell the way you do tonight," He said.

She smiled at him and decided that even though she did not really know this man, she would trust him. How could she not, the horses trusted him.

"I didn't mean to grab you like that, Lenora. You looked so lovely in the starlight, and I've wanted to give you a little kiss for a while now. I didn't think it would be that kind of kiss to begin with but I guess…" he trailed off.

"It's okay. I liked it. If you couldn't tell," Lenora said.

Clay pulled her to his chest and she rested her head against his shoulder. He smelled wonderful; not of jasmine, but of horses and pine trees and maybe some saddle soap. Had she ever known a man to smell so delightful? Never. The men in her life before smelled like Armani; artificial.

"You know the first day you pulled in I couldn't believe my eyes. I thought, 'who is this goddess driving a truck and trailer? And she just changed a flat tire? What can't this girl do? Is it crazy that I'm so attracted to a girl because she drives a truck, rides a horse and looks amazing while doing it?'" Clay said.

He was laughing and Lenora found herself laughing too. Then he bent his head and nuzzled at her lips with his, barely brushing them. Her panties were wet and her legs weak. This man had done something crazy to her, and she blamed the stars and the mountain as well. Best wingmen a guy could ask for, she thought. Even Major had helped. She felt her hands wander up his chest, enjoying the play of muscles. She knew she could not wait to get his shirt off and feel his skin under her fingertips. For now, though, she just twisted her fingers in his hair and kissed him, letting his hand press the small of her back into the whole strength of him.

CHAPTER FOUR

Lenora woke up with a light, tingly feeling in her stomach. What had happened last night? Oh, yes. Clay had happened. Her mind brought back the clear, dark sky filled with millions of stars, the mountains still, and yet awake with the night and Clay. She felt him again; his hands when he pulled her off the horse. His touch had been, like nothing she ever felt before. She had to hide her burning face; the thoughts going through her mind were way too much. What would she do to this man? Or maybe the better question would be; what would she not do to this man, given the chance? She tried to remember back to her ex-husband, she could not find the same sensation of pure desire in her memory. Had she ever felt so aroused? It was not even the arousal though, it was something more, a sort of deep attraction that seemed to draw her into him and the mountains and horses. Was this man somehow connected to the very energetic wholeness of Bear Dance Ranch and the mountains? She knew the horses felt a deep sense of safety and rightness when they were with him, and she felt the same way. It was as if he would not wrong her any more than a boulder on the mountain or a branch on a spruce.

Well, could she really trust this feeling? She had been

misled by men before, yes, this was true, but more than that she had been deluded by her own heart. That was truly the worst feeling in the world. Her very own heart had led her into a very painful relationship where nothing good had come. Was that really true though? She had learned some things about herself; she had learned not to be so trusting. Lenora wished, not for the first time, that her mother had shared a little more about her own experiences with Lenora's father.

What must that have been like for her mother to have left the man who fathered her? She had left behind her whole family as she moved east to the city and slowly forged a new life for herself. That must have taken spunk, will and determination, Lenora thought. Her mother truly was an inspiration; she had raised Lenora, put herself through college and a master's degree program, then directed a very prominent theater company. She was a woman who had not looked back with regret, Lenora thought, but now that she was gone Lenora realized there were so many things she had never gotten around to asking her mother.

She found herself wondering if perhaps her own mother, whom she imagined as a combination of Superwoman and Charlotte Bronte, might have in fact made a mistake with a guy, Lenora's cowboy dad, and, having chosen wrongly, or at least having trusted her heart and been led astray, if she had decided to stop trusting. Was this what her mother felt? Was that not the worst human thing possible, to stop trusting one's own instincts? It seemed so hugely unfair that her own mother had never been able to move beyond her man-mistake and trust and love again.

Lenora rolled over in bed, sober with the thoughts of her own life's twisted journey and what she was learning along the way. She felt a little guilty questioning her own mother's motives to not open her heart again after the sad failure with Lenora's father. Should she question her mother who had so obviously been successful in life? Was having a wonderful job, well raised child and lovely home enough to compensate for never really giving love another chance?

Then she had the very sad thought, maybe it's just a fling for Clay? Or even worse; maybe it was nothing at all. Maybe he was just lonely and bored. Who knows with that man, just because he's good with horses does not make him the perfect boyfriend. She had heard plenty of stories from her mother about the cowboys with their girlfriends in each town. Perhaps he thought she was just here at the ranch for a little stay and it would be fun to have a quick romance.

She sighed, enough thinking in bed, the day had started without her, and there was a great deal to do before hungry people would be expecting breakfast. Lenora knew her personal weakness was her own ability to overthink life, love and everything in-between.

After breakfast, while cleaning horse stalls— she always had her best insight while cleaning up after these messy animals— she realized that she did not really care if the cowboy was just playing her. She was going to be as brave as she could, given the circumstances, and just follow the sweet breath of mountain air and see what came of this thing that was stirring between them.

At that moment Clay came down the aisle of the barn with a sweaty horse and a big smile for her. He swept his hat off, and, after checking that no one was looking, he swooped down for a kiss that made Lenora unable to wipe the silly smile from her face.

"Would you go away with me for a few days?" Clay said.

"Where?" Lenora said.

"There's a three or four day ride up into the mountains. It winds around some. But we could check the fence in the north pasture and also along the alpine meadows," Clay said. "For the summer grazing, you know?"

"Yes," Lenora said.

The single word answer had left her mouth before she even realized that she wanted to go. Well, so much for being careful!

"I'll speak to your uncle about it. I know he wants me to

get up there to check the fence pretty soon anyway," Clay said. He looked down at his boots for a moment. "Glad you're coming this year." He said the last part quickly, his voice a low rush of words.

Then he led his horse off to get a bath. Lenora went back to cleaning her stall, feeling a little dizzy. After chores she went in the house to get another cup of coffee and found Annie sitting at her desk with a letter in her lap. As soon as Lenora appeared her aunt pushed the letter under a stack of papers.

"What's wrong?" Lenora said.

"Nothing we haven't faced before." Annie looked grim.

She did not elaborate and Lenora poured herself the last cup of coffee and started another pot, knowing the men would be coming in soon enough for refills.

"You know, I have a little money from selling mom's house. Maybe I can help?" Lenora said.

"Oh, no. It will be fine. We always get through these rough spots. We haven't reached the point yet where we have to become one of *those* dude ranches or sell to the developers," Annie said.

Lenora blew on her coffee to cool it, and then added a teaspoon of coconut oil to the cup. She was right to assume that her aunt and uncle were having money trouble. She could only imagine how expensive the taxes alone must be on this big of a spread. A dude ranch? What would that be like, she thought.

Looking out the kitchen window Lenora saw the old bunkhouses with their rusted roofs and log exteriors, bleached nearly white from the wind and cold, with new eyes. She knew how trendy it was to stay in the mountains on a real, working ranch and eat beef from the ranges, ride horses, hike, go rock climbing. She wondered how bad exactly the finances were. Really, it was not her place to try and step in with a solution. Who knew how long she would even stay at the ranch? Her throat tightened with the thought of trying to go back to her old life. Well, going back was not an option;

her old life was pretty well gone, no mother, no husband and no job. She took a large gulp of coffee to get her mind off the past. Bear Dance Ranch, here, now, this was her life. She would help with the money problems if they would let her.

***

That night at dinner, as the large, gluten-free yeast rolls that Lenora had baked that afternoon were passed around the table, Clay brought up the trip.

"I think I need to head up and check those fences. Better do it now before we start moving the herds to the summer pastures. I'd like to take Lenora with me and show her the real beauty of this place," Clay said.

Lenora thought she saw a look pass between her aunt and uncle, but was not sure if her overactive imagination was responsible for her suspicion or not. She kept her own head down and concentrated on her roasted Brussel sprouts and baby portabellas. It was strange to feel like a teenager sneaking out on a date. Not that this was a date! She hurried to stifle that thought before anything else could come of it.

"That sounds about perfect. We've got all the calves on the ground and it's about time to let them eat some fresh, green grass. When will you go?" Uncle Byron said.

"We better go tomorrow, there's clear weather up at the pass for the next few days, don't know when that might change," Clay said.

"Bring lots of layers. You never know when it might snow," Annie said. "Will you take Major? Is he ready?"

"He's ready," both Lenora and Clay said at the same time.

Lenora wondered if her aunt and uncle heard the floorboards creak as she snuck out of the house at night for her moonlight adventures. Should she just tell them? But really, there was nothing to tell! She was a grown-ass woman who had kissed a grown-ass man, and that was it. It was not like they were getting married or even dating.

CHRISTINA RHOADS

CHAPTER FIVE

The air had taken on a crisp edge, purple shadows stretched in front of the horses and every boulder seemed twice as large as it should be.

"Up ahead is a perfect campsite. We should probably stop for the night," Clay said.

He turned and looked at her and for a brief moment their eyes met and she felt herself an open book for him to read—this scared her. After all, she could not help but think that feeling so crazy for a man like him could not end well. He seemed to be reading her mind because he glanced over at her again and smiled that lopsided grin where only one side of his mouth pulled up before speaking.

"Race you to the top of that hill?" Clay said.

They cantered the horses up the top of the next prominence and she found a natural circle of large stones, some quite tall. There was also thick grass for the horses. It was indeed the perfect campsite. As she slid from Major's back and slipped the bridle and saddle from him, she felt lightheaded and tongue-tied. She worked silently brushing the sweat marks from Major's coat, enjoying the way his glossy hair caught the rays of the dying sun. With each stroke of her hand her horse's hair turned platinum, copper and silver-gold.

She wanted nothing more than to spend time with this mysterious man, and yet she could not string together two words now that they were alone. He was attending to his own mare and only once the horse had been untacked, groomed and hobbled did he approach Lenora and Major.

"Do you want me to put the hobbles on for tonight?" Clay said.

His hands were at his sides and the palms were turned towards her in the unthreatening way he used with the young horses he trained. She wondered if she looked frightened to him. Or maybe he too felt it? How could he not. Every time their hands touched even for the briefest second she felt as if she had laid her palm on the hot wood stove. He held her gaze, and she realized that he was waiting for her reply. She looked down quickly and felt her cheeks grow hot.

"Yes, please help. I'm, I'm still an English rider I guess," she said. "I'm trying to figure out all this cowboy stuff and sometimes it seems like so much…"

She was rambling now. It was as if she either could not speak at all or had to babble like a bubbling steam.

Glancing up in time, she saw his eyes grow so soft and gentle. She felt all the air leave her body quickly and silently— she was as light as a poof of dandelion white. He took the two steps that separated them in one stride. With the same gentleness as when he first haltered a new colt, he brushed his palm along her cheek his thumb touching her lips.

"I love the color you turn," he said. His voice was deep, and his hand trembled just a little.

Lenora could not draw in air. With the same gentleness his hand slid away and he knelt showing her the careful twist of the hobble. This was in order to keep Major from wandering too far, while still allowing him to enjoy all the fresh grass around their camp.

Next, Clay moved off to gather wood for the fire and Lenora made makeshift beds from their blanket rolls and gathered together the food supplies. Several apples, some dates and a bag of almonds and then a half loaf of bread and hunk of cheese plus two big potatoes and two ears of corn. It was nearly dark when he came back; whistling softly and stopping to let a curious Major sniff the bundle of wood he carried. He held up two still dripping trout, for Lenora's inspection, his grin both proud and confident. Lenora pulled together dry grass and mounded stones to form a fireplace.

He knelt and nodded at the fireplace. "Not bad for an Easterner." His eyes were teasing.

She could see that lopsided smile again though his face was nearly hidden in the shadow of darkening evening. His teeth shone white for just a minute and she felt her stomach tighten as he flicked the lighter, nursing the tiny flame into the bundle of grasses she had prepared.

Once the fire was strong, he showed her how to soak the corn in water and tie the shucks together and then rake a bed of coals, in which to cook the food. He said little, but when he spoke his voice was low and musical and she felt a little helpless as if he was somehow herding her, guiding her to someplace she hoped was safe. She supposed this was how his horses felt at first, not knowing if this was a human they could trust, yet hoping, against all hope— against the past really— that this was the *one* to trust.

They ate hot food, the smoke from the fire spiraling straight up into the clear, star-studded sky. The food filled her belly and she found herself nestling into her blanket roll feeling safe. He began to hum a little tune and then sang a ballad in Spanish that sounded sad and beautiful all at once. Lenora surprised herself when she lifted her voice in the old church hymn her mother had taught her. As her voice rose and drifted off in the clear air she realized she felt as safe as she had ever been.

When she fell silent, he spoke quietly. "I could listen to your voice, under these stars, forever."

A shiver ran up her spine, she watched as he ran his hand through his hair, tucking the ends behind his ears. He was facing away from her, towards the fire and the night, and when he turned back she could not read all that was in his face, because he blocked the light from the fire. But what she did see scared her. There was depth to this man. He took her hand in his and brought her knuckles to his lips. His eyes were dark and never left her face, asking permission she realized. He must have seen it because he bent his head and she felt his lips brush hers. Sparks surely hissed between them she thought. His hand cradled her face. He was the one to pull away and she watched his profile in the flickering light as he ran his hand through his hair again. When he turned back towards her his face was once again half in shadow but his words were earnest:

"It's crazy to, to feel this way. I'm not really a kid anymore and wasn't expecting to meet someone and feel out of control. Are you the White Buffalo woman my people speak of?"

She knew she should say something in return but she was frightened suddenly. Wrapping her blanket tightly around her shoulders she leaned away hoping the shadows would hide her own face.

"I don't know." She kept it simple.

Frightened, was an understatement. She wanted this, whatever *this* was but also felt her insides curl up with fear at what this man might end up meaning to her.

"We don't really know each other," he said. "My wife." There was a long pause, and she felt her shoulders tighten even further.

"My, ex-wife and I knew each other nearly our whole adult lives."

She must have been holding her breath, because, once released, it came out like a gasp.

"You didn't know I was married before? Surely you asked around?" He sounded confused.

"Who would I ask? I've been the ranch hermit since coming out here! I guess you asked around?" Lenora said.

"Well, yes. I… you were the beautiful niece," he replied.

She mulled that over that one word: beautiful.

"How long were you married?"

"Longer than I should have been." He paused: "She works down at Carl's, you've probably seen her."

Lenora had seen her with dark hair swinging down her back, and lovely silver bracelets on each wrist. She worked at the tack store that also was a diner , the only one for miles and miles. Her name tag had read: *Crystal.* Lenora remembered how quick her smile was for all the cowboys in the place.

There were ghosts out in the dark and Lenora realized she had brought them with her. The past could be clung to or released: her choice. As if proving her thoughts valid a lone coyote cried from the ridge across from their tiny fire.

"I'll water the horses again and get another log for the fire," Clay said.

"Thank you. I mean thank you, for bringing me," Lenora said.

He stood over her for a second and smiled that lopsided grin before walking into the dark.

"The pleasure's all mine. Ma'am," he said.

She laughed and waited for him to leave before peeing behind one of the big rocks.

She must have fallen asleep before he returned, because she remembered only seeing his shadowed back towards her as he stoked the fire. Much later she woke cold and stiff, the fire was burning down to gray ash and orange coals. She shifted in her blankets trying to get warm. She could hear his even breaths and wanted to drift off herself, but decided to try and pee again. As she returned to her blankets, he said: "Cold?"

"Yes," she replied.

As she burrowed into her blankets he stood and shook out his ground roll next to hers. Then spread his blankets on top of her stiff, chilled body and slipped in behind her. He was wearing a cotton shirt and some type of trousers; he nestled into her back and very, very carefully wrapped his arm around her. Her breathing went quick at first, but, as the warmth from his body and the added blankets spread through her, she soon forgot the thrill of having this man in her bed and relaxed. Thankful to be warm she drifted in the haze of the dream world.

Just at the brink of sleep she imagined that he bent his face into the crook of her neck and kissed her.

She woke to the warmth of sunlight on her face. The sky to the east was a glorious tapestry of impossible pinks and brilliant orange. Major and Dark Moon were close by, grazing as the sun rose beside them. Clay was adding kindling to the fire, coaxing the flames back to life.

"Sleep well?" He said.

He looked amazing; his cotton shirt was unbuttoned halfway showing his dark, sculpted chest. He must have just washed in the river, because his hair was wet, and his face was glowing a warm copper from the cold.

"Yes, I did," Lenora said. She smiled at him and felt alive and very well. "I think I'll go wash up down at the river too."

She slipped out of the blankets and grabbed her towel and a bar of soap. The water was icy and so refreshing. Modestly, she went down to where the banks were steepest and hid her body from his view. But she could not help imagining stripping down with his eyes on her. She scrubbed until her body was glowing pink and alive, she mapped the freckles across her chest and arms. As she dressed she was surprised at how she felt as if the rest of her life was before her, like the rest of her life was her own. For so long the past had been more real than either the present or future.

When she returned to camp, he had two of the fillets crisp and an apple sliced. They ate in companionable silence until he spoke.

"Do you want to keep going? It's another two days to do the whole loop," he said.

Her whole body wanted to answer for her, *yes!* It screamed. She had wanted this adventure since she was a child, since she read the *Black Stallion*, since she could first ride her horse down a quiet trail. And now to do it with this hunk of a man? Yes, of course, she thought.

"Sure," she said.

She looked up at him. She imagined her *yes!!* with the double exclamation marks was plain to read. He smiled, and she felt a little light headed.

"You're the prettiest thing I've ever seen in the morning," Clay said. He spoke without the hint of a smile, but his eyes were dancing. He bent and kissed her on the cheek.

They packed their dwindling supplies and then saddled the horses. The sun had barely brushed the tops of the hills to the east as they headed out from their makeshift camp.

As they rode, she imagined ways to ask about his ex-wife and how he had ended up working at the ranch. Why was he so good with horses? How old was he. Thirty-five? She really did not know. She thought he would tell but she was not sure she was brave enough to ask. Major seemed more than happy to keep going, he was prancing a little under her seat and she steadied him with a pat to his neck. He just tossed his head and then flicked his long, white tail up over his back. The flamboyant, Arabian style that was his heritage was really coming through this morning.

"Want to canter?" She was grinning uncontrollably as she asked.

He shot a red, hot smile right back at her. "You're on!"

Before she knew it they were off. Major felt strong and sure under her, and oh-so-fast. She stood up just a little in the stirrups and bent down to his neck and let the wind wash over her face as the sheer joy of a gallop on a fine morning became her whole life. The world was waking up to the glorious, spring day and all around them trees began to sprout and tiny streams of melting snow made way for fresh, green grass. The trail wound up and away to the mountain pass and both horses felt the joy of the moment, ears back against their heads and necks thrown out as their shoulders rolled with power. A herd of elk, startled by the galloping horses and riders, lifted their heads and watched, thick mouthfuls of grass trapped in their heavy jaws.

The horses finally slowed and when she looked at Clay, he smiled that grin she was growing to love so much. His eyes were bright with the wind and the joy of the morning. She felt a deep sigh escape her body, and she knew that the past was being healed on this journey. As the horses relaxed into a leisurely walk, she felt a deep well of words come to the surface and she began to tell him about the *bad time*.

Lenora and her mother had been more like sisters than parent and child. Maura was young when she had Lenora. Only eighteen and with her blond curls, tiny wrists and round eyes she seemed much younger than her age. Maura had been a dancer and actor and her life revolved around the stage and the dramas on and off it. Lenora spent the first years of her life backstage watching flustered ballerinas rush about in various stages of undress. When Lenora turned ten her mother made the difficult decision and moved the two of them from New York City to Chicago for a steady, theater management position. Maura gave up her own onstage dreams, but found her power as a calm force for achieving all the necessary action done behind the scenes. Lenora stayed in the same school and began as a working student at a local horse barn. They had built a life together. Lenora had not realized how much her mother treated her as an equal until she was older and saw the horrible fights her teenage friends had with their stressed parents. Somehow, she had assumed that all parents and children operated as an efficient team. Perhaps, this was one of the many reasons that it had hurt so bad when her mother kept the diagnosis from her for so long. Six months was a long time to keep a secret of such magnitude from the only other person on one's team, Lenora reasoned.

Holding and nursing the illness, Maura had gone from slim and muscular to a skeleton. Lenora confronted her mother as they sat eating a long overdue dinner together.

"Why didn't you tell me before?" Lenora said.

"Darling, I couldn't bring it up before now, there was too much going on with.... With your marriage," Maura said.

Maura met Lenora's eyes as the truth of the future ahead began to become clear.

Lenora swallowed down the bitter taste left behind from her failed marriage; her mother had never thought Mick was quite right for her, though Maura had kept quiet about this for the most part. Somehow her laughable, relationship was to blame for the loss of six, precious months with her mother.

Lenora set down her napkin and started to cry; her mother stood and hugged her, letting Lenora's face hide in the thick folds of her purple cardigan. They left the restaurant and Lenora knew that her world had shifted in a new and sudden way; there was before the evening of May 15th and there was after.

The days drug on; then randomly, suddenly, picked up speed. Weeks slipped past as a single afternoon spent reading to her mother in the downstairs bedroom, the afternoon sun slanting through the half-closed blinds. Lenora found herself pulling away from her outside life; before she knew it, she had somehow been fired from her job and was two months behind on rent. The only thing she kept up with was her morning routine at the barn where Major was boarded. She moved into her mother's house so that she could care for her. The days began to flow into a long goodbye. During the last weeks, Maura was in hospice care. Lenora knew the long goodbye was over. For the first time, she began to realize she would be alone. She was scared suddenly on a purely personal level. As she spent the last hours with her mother, she found herself filled with a deep fear for her own future. How could she worry about herself when her mother was in horrible pain beside her? She felt so human and so flawed, the world closed in as her courage fled. Consciousness slipped from her mother, and Lenora found herself losing all control and pleading with Maura not to leave her. Lenora held her mother's wing-boned hand and sobbed with no hope of comfort in the future to come.

Major snorted and swished his tail. Lenora looked down at his mane and let the stiff breeze dry the tears trapped in her eyelashes. She could feel Clay was listening even though he had been completely silent during her whole telling. Glancing at him, she saw that his eyes were on her and his face held the same softness she had glimpsed last night. She took a deep breath and continued; there really was nothing else to do.

The funeral, in Lenora's memory, was a horrid whirl of friends and family, all trying to say uplifting things. How shallow their attempts at comfort sounded from the mud of her despair.

Her aunt and uncle came, her mother's sister Annie with her husband Byron, whom Lenora and her mother had visited once in Montana. They stood close to Lenora throughout all the greetings and condolences. Annie was her mother's older sister and her husband Byron was a man that waves could break upon, even the sad ones. It was Byron who first asked her to move west with them to the mountains. Byron, she realized, must have seen the true depth of her growing depression. Annie's face had come alive with her husband's suggestion and she had held Lenora's hand so hard that it began to go numb.

Still, it had taken Lenora eleven months to load her horse on the trailer and head west. Sometimes, deep mud is a hard thing to escape.

Lenora fell silent as she fully descended back into the moment, and was once again astride her horse riding into the mountain wilds. As she spoke of her dark time aloud, with Clay and the horses as her witnesses, she released that time of its power over her and sent it on its way, carried by the west wind. Clay reached out his hand across the empty space separating their horses and touched her arm. When she looked up and met his eyes, she was shocked to see such deep sadness. She wondered for a moment if the pain in her heart was somehow reflected into his. There were lines in his open face which she had never seen before. Not for the first time, she realized that her own pain was only a drop in the whole ocean of world hurts. What heaviness did Clay carry over his own heart, she wondered.

They rode on in silence as the clouds overhead thickened and spun from white to gray to lavender. A skittish wind kicked up its heels.

"I think we might get some kind of storm." Clay glanced again over his shoulder at the darkening sky.

"Where can we go?" Lenora felt very much from the city and wanted the comfort of buildings and other people. After her emotional unburdening, she felt tired and in need of warmth and care.

"Don't worry." He smiled. "Up ahead. You see that line of cliffs?"

Yes, she could see them and they did not seem too far ahead. Just through the bowl of the valley and then up.

"We'll head there. And make camp in one of the old caves." Clay said. He sounded confident and like perhaps he had done it before.

"Ok." Lenora tried to make her voice sound brave.

Would there be rattlesnakes in caves like that, she wondered. She did not know, and really did not want to let her imagination get the best of her.

He glanced again at the darkening sky and said, "We better trot a little."

The horses seemed happy to pick up the pace, as the wind blew their tails sideways and flattened the grass around them. After twenty-five minutes and a little galloping, they reached the cliffs and dismounted. Clay searched for the opening to the cave, as the wind began to toss small sticks and icy pellets. Lenora felt her heart begin to race as the wind made the horses hard to hold, and the frozen bits began to mix with hard-driven rain.

"Here it is," Clay said.

A large boulder partially covered the entrance to a cave, which was tall enough for even the horses to enter. A lightning bolt crashed through the sky, and the heavens opened drenching horses and humans alike. Quickly, they stepped into the eerie darkness of the cave.

It was huge, maybe thirty or forty feet high. Once they hurried through the opening, Lenora realized it was very deep. She rested her wet face against Major's damp, but warm shoulder, relieved to be out of the storm.

"This way," Clay said.

He moved into the darkness, and Lenora had no choice but to follow him. The cave opened up before them and the darkness overhead indicated huge expanse. She could still hear the storm, and when she looked back to the mouth of the cave, spider lightning shot across the dark sky. She turned back and Clay was standing next to her. He touched her shoulder and she realized she was starting to shiver in her wet clothes.

"Are you okay?" Clay said. "We need to get you out of those clothes and by a warm fire."

He took over, unpacking the horses and securing them in the back of the cave. He laid out some dried sticks and struck a match and had a small fire going all by the time Lenora struggled with her cold hands to undo the swollen straps on her saddle bags.

"Come here, are you okay?" Clay asked again.

She realized she must look bad to have him so worried.

"Yes, just really cold," Lenora said.

"Come here. I'll help you," Clay said.

He laid down a bedroll, pulled Lenora's boots off. Then stood her on the blankets before stripping her out of her wet jeans and layered sweaters. Quickly, he threw a blanket around her shoulders and then stood, stripping out of his own wet clothes. Her breathing quickened as he pulled free of his damp shirt, and the firelight lit his skin to a dark, rich copper in the ever-shifting light. She reached out her cold, stiff hand and touched his chest. He caught her hand and looked down at her and his eyes were dark but the flames from the fire reflected a deep, deep desire.

"Careful, Nora," he said.

She reached her other hand up and touched his dark hair, still dripping from the rain. She did not want to be careful. He caught this hand too and pulled both behind her back so that she was his captive, her wet body pressed against his. He bent his head and kissed her. This kiss was different; this was not the same man who had chastely warmed her last night with his extra blankets and his lean body. This man was alive and hot with desire and she could feel he wanted her in a primal way which made her pulse race. He was rough as he kissed her, his lips hot and raw from the wind and their earlier gallop to safety. She was emboldened and bit his lower lip; she heard his growl, deep in his throat. He released one of her hands to run his thumb under her chin, holding her head more firmly in position as he deepened the kiss further. She bent back away from him, even as their bodies became closer, her skin had gone from icy cold to burning hot and she wanted to feel all of him. With her one free hand she struggled with the sodden belt buckle on his pants and tried to free him. He was kissing along her jawline, down her throat, his hand moving from her neck to her hair, he knotted his fists in her wet curls.

"Do you want this? Nora, tell me?" Clay said. "Tell me now, or I won't be able to stop."

"Yes," she struggled to speak.

"Yes what?" Clay said.

"I want you." Her voice sounded strange even to her own ears: raspy, full of lust.

With that, he pulled her down to the blankets, rough, eager, peeling her out of her wet sports bra. He bent his head and took her left nipple into his mouth and twirled his tongue in slow circles making her knot both her fists in his hair and gasp. He lifted his head and kissed her, hard, his tongue making the same circles inside her mouth. When he drew away her eyes were glazed, and he smiled with pleasure.

His skin was soft with a small, crescent-moon shaped scar on his chest, which was so sexy she had to lift her head and taste it, taking in his scent of mountains, horses and wood smoke. A trail of darker hair led down his belly into the waistband of his well-worn jeans, and, when her hands eagerly reached to unbutton them, he stopped her there.

"Baby, don't go too fast." He was almost pleading. His mouth was just as ravenous as he kissed her, pushing her back down. The firelight flickered across his tanned chest as he stroked her smooth sides and up to her breasts. He ran his finger inside the band of her pale, blue panties. Only once he had slipped his hand back out and was kissing her neck, could she struggle again with the buckle on his jeans. The backs of her hands savored the feel of hair from his stomach and the taunt muscle underneath. This was a man who used his body each day riding colts; he was a dance partner with wild horses. The feel of him turned her insides into pure desire. She peeled his jeans back and ran her hands under the soft fabric of his briefs. His skin was silk. He moaned as her hands touched him.

"Darling." He whispered against her hair as her hands shyly touched the first soft skin of his erection. She could feel all of him pressed against her hip and wanted nothing more than to hold the fullness of him in her hands. He was kissing her again and stroking with his own hand, making her wet and crazy and leaving her gasping with the delve of his fingers. His kisses grew longer, traveling sometimes to her throat and others times to her shoulders and stomach, until she could not think of anything except the heavy feel of his largeness on her and the throbbing of her lotus. He cupped her face in both his hands, kissing her fully, deeply. And then rolled away, searching, she realized, in the pocket of his jeans. He came back with a packet and she smiled, feeling safe and warm, her body tingling with joy at both his thoughtfulness and his huge erection eager for her. She sat up resting on one elbow and watched unabashedly as he slid the condom on. She felt a little chill run up her back, as thoughts of what she was going to let this cowboy do to her ran through her mind.

He was so gentle now, kissing her as he slid into her soft folds. He stopped to let her adjust to all of him and waited until she had wrapped both her legs around his body, deepening the position before he thrust, feeling her, not rushing. She was wet and open. She whimpered, burning, her face in his neck.

He whispered into her ear, his breath warm, "I'd love to have you sit astride me. But it's been a long while for me and I'm barely holding on as it is."

His honesty moved her and she laid still, letting him work her body slowly, stopping when he came close. He even withdrew, leaving her cold and empty to run his fingers over her clit, stroking her in circular motions until she was wild and about to fall off the cliff of desire, then he entered her again. The thrusts more vigorous now, she slid her hand down to touch herself and let his body forcing against her hand bringher to the brink of climax. She slid her hand away and felt him hard and thick against her as she came with a gasping cry loud enough to reach the roof of the cave. He said something sweet and nonsensical in her ear and then they were both still.

CHAPTER SIX

Outside the cave she could hear the rain had slowed to a steady patter. The horses moved, restless behind the fire. Clay ran his fingers through her hair. Her nose felt numb and her whole body tingly. She could see questions in his eyes but did not know what they were. He reached his hand out and brushed along her cheekbones.

"I love the firelight in your hair," he said. His eyes were soft, and she reached out and touched his shoulder, wanting to feel his skin under her fingers.

Her mind was full of so many thoughts; the past, the future. Taking a deep breath she released it slowly, she wanted to just enjoy the firelight and this gorgeous man. She took another deep breath and quieted her mind. She was here, in this cave, now. When she opened her eyes, he was still watching her.

"Want to do it again?" His smile was there and his eyes were dancing. She laughed and leaned forward to kiss him.

"We better let the horses out for some grass," She said.

"I'll take them."

"Okay. But no clothes." She was smiling now.

"I'll freeze out there!" He said.

"Okay, okay. You can wear your boots and hat."

She watched the whole time as he led the horses out of the cave in his boots and nothing else. The horses did not seem to notice, though she imagined that they knew what the two humans had been doing. She felt a bit like a mom caught with a dad and kind of liked it.

When he came back to bed, he was indeed cold and wet; she ran her hands over the length of him, amazed again at the strength in his thighs and delicious abs. She licked the smooth line between his pectoral muscles and breathed in the scent of horses and leather. His skin tasted salty on her tongue.

"I want you again," Clay said. Burying his face in her hair he positioned her so that she sat astride him, her chestnut locks a wild mane down her back and half covering her breasts.

***

She slipped out of bed before him. He sleepily touched her hip and leg as she pulled free of the warm nest of blankets. Outside with only her jacket and a towel and bar of soap she made her way to the river. Mist rose from the water in the chill morning air. She stopped to pat Major's shoulder and give him a good morning kiss on his velvety nose. The water was even colder than she expected but woke her up better than a cup of coffee. A great blue heron was wading in the shallows at the bend in the river. She watched its slow walk, interrupted by long pauses, before it caught a silvery minnow and ate it in one swallow.

As she greeted the morning, she wondered why it had taken her so long to come west. She supposed all the figurative doors in her old life closing at once had left her a little shell-shocked. Of course, she should have come as soon as her mother died. Hindsight was like that, the path clear and easy to discern. She was starting to realize life was not lived in the past. Funny, how her mother's death had illuminated something she had secretly known for a while;

her marriage had not been even close to functional. In fact, her ex-husband was a bit of a jerk, and she wondered how she had fallen for him in the first place. She knew it was because she had made the mistake of believing his need to control her meant he loved her.

Spending the night with Clay was bringing up more memories than she had expected. Her ex-husband had been a man who thought he could "break" Lenora. Not in any physical way, but just in his attempts to mold her into the type of woman to whom he saw himself married. When she had been studying clean eating and vegetarian cooking methods in culinary school, he had singly-mindedly gone about convincing her that she should study the mainstays of cooking, since these were sure to land her a "safe job" in a large kitchen, he had argued. He was right in some ways; she had landed a job with a large chain restaurant right out of school. Instead of being able to experiment and try her own exciting culinary creations, she had to follow detailed recipes to create tried and true menu items day after day. Simply put, she was dying inside every moment of every day. Each time she gave into Mick's steady direction for her life, she gave up on her own creative impulses. Soon enough these urges began to get quieter and quieter, like the cries of a tiny child lost inside the dark well of her life. Her spirit was tired and giving out. She found herself unable to make a decision without consulting Mick first.

Her mother had seen what was going on and tried to intervene. Both embarrassed and confused, Lenora's response had been to shut her mother out of her life except for a few stilted phone conversations and hurried lunches. Perhaps, that was why her mother had waited so long to reveal her sickness. The news of her mother's illness had shaken Lenora out of her zombie daze and made her realize she was not living anything resembling the life of her dreams.

The blue heron spread its massive wings and silently flew upriver, bringing Lenora back from the past. The rising sun bathed the world in liquid gold and the smell of spring grass and river mud filled the new day. Never before had she been more thankful to be on the other side of such a hard period in her life. Alone, wrapped in nothing but her towel, she sat on a blanket on the river bank. She felt him approach, his footsteps were even and nearly silent, he knelt behind her and enfolded her in his arms.

He smelled like smoke from the fire and sweat that made her skin tingle and nostrils flare. He felt like part of the peace. She leaned back into his arms and watched the steam rise from the river.

"How did you sleep?" His lips brushed her neck.

"Perfectly," she responded. Her neck tingled from his nearness.

"Me too," Clay said. "I imagine we were worn out from all that exercise."

She turned in his arms to see his quick smile; he bent and kissed her on the lips.

Gently, he unwrapped his arms from around her. She tried to not watch him undress before he headed to the river, but her eyes seemed to have a mind of their own.

"Have you no shame?"

He playfully wiggled a behind that was a shade lighter than the rest of him, but oh, wow, was it a well-made one.

She blushed and went to prepare some breakfast.

After they had eaten and washed the dishes in the river, they sat outside the cave and watched the horses graze in the eastern slanting sunlight.

"How long is the ride home?" she asked, looking at the ground.

"Four hours," he said.

Her greatest fear was losing the feeling of freedom she felt pulsing out from her heart into her arms and legs. How long had it been since she had felt this way, she wondered? Maybe, it was falling in love again. She almost gasped aloud upon thinking the *L* word, but managed to keep it to herself. Whatever *it* was, was so much more than just lust. Everything felt so right out here with the big sky, open range, wind, horses and life all around her.

She looked up from the blade of grass she had been pulling apart while lost in thought and saw his eyes on her. He reached his hand out and tucked a loose wisp of hair behind her ear.

"Ready to go home?" His eyes were kind.

She could see him searching her face for clues as to what she was thinking. She tried to smile. "Yes." She wanted to assure him that something healing had happened for her out on the range, under the stars, even while she did not yet fully comprehend it herself.

It did feel good to hear him say 'home' and picture her aunt and uncle's rambling old house, even if she would have liked to stay out longer, to live outside the rules and the pressures of ordinary life. What could she do to feel this free every day, she wondered. Make love to Clay, she thought to herself and then smiled, imagining him tiptoeing past her uncle's bedroom door every morning.

They were quiet on most of the ride; the morning fading into a beautiful midday, the sky a blue so deep she imagined it was like the sea with depths and depths of hidden wonders above its surface. Her legs were tired and she realized despite the cold river baths she was ready for some warm water and lavender scented conditioner for her tangled hair. But how would it be between her and Clay? He was riding ahead of her; she watched his straight back and the graceful drape of his legs around the barrel of his mare. She was not sure how she should act around him with the busy ranch around them and the crush of everyday life. Dinner around the big table, her aunt and uncle, there were so many variables. Was she his girlfriend, she wondered. She was not naïve enough to think that just because they spent the night together they were destined to be together forever, but there was softness to his face when he touched her, gentleness. What did it all mean to him?

He must have been reading her mind, because he circled his mare back and rode beside her.

"You're quiet," he said.

"Yes," she said. Sorry."

She did not know how to voice her question without feeling silly. On the one hand, she did not want him to feel like he owed her anything, but she did want to know how *he* felt. She was an adult woman who had made a willing choice last night and had enjoyed herself a great deal. Yet, she was immensely attracted to Clay and wanted to forge some type of relationship with him if she could. Also, there was the tiny kernel of fear that Clay might have some dark, past secrets or personality flaws that made him a true bad boy, and so perhaps that was why she was so attracted to him. After a mistake like her ex, Mick, it was going to be hard to trust her own instincts again.

"Do you have plans Saturday?" He asked.

She felt herself grinning and could not help it.

"Well, I'll have to look at my calendar when I get home. What day is it?" She asked.

"I think Tuesday. But I've been sleeping under the stars with a beautiful woman for too many nights and may have lost count!" Clay said.

She hugged the promise of Saturday night to her heart for the rest of the ride home.

They rode at a steady trot until they reached the big hill overlooking the ranch. Instinctually, they both stopped and sat atop their horses gazing out at the ranch spread below them with barns, farmhouse, corrals and pasture, the green irrigated grass and the brown of dust mixed in as well. She realized looking down into the valley that it was home. She smiled to herself feeling a joy she had not known in a long time. Beside her, the horseman was quiet, and when she looked at him his face was brooding and eyes shadowed with things she did not know.

"Are you ready to go back?" She asked.

"Yes," Clay said. "But I won't lie and say that I don't sometimes wish I didn't have to."

His reply left her feeling oddly disturbed, she would have asked him to clarify, but at that moment a dog far below spotted them and let out welcoming a bark. It was time to ride down and rejoin humanity. As they descended from the heights, she glanced back over her shoulder once and said a silent prayer of thanks to the range for letting her have some time to heal in the soothing realness of nature.

As Lenora banged into the ranch kitchen, Annie met her with a huge hug. Her aunt was dressed in jeans and a sleeveless green knit shirt. Her arms were muscled and tanned, with tiny freckles dotting nearly every inch of exposed skin. Annie was often mistaken for a woman in her forties not sixties, and today was no exception.

"Welcome home, Dear," Annie said.

Her embrace felt warm, and for the first time since coming west, Lenora felt herself relax into the other woman's arms without having to fight off guilt. Guilt was a sneaky little thing; she found it trying to make her feel bad for beginning to live her life again. It was hard enough to imagine she would in fact be okay, despite no longer having her mother; guilt did not help.

"You're just in time to help me with dinner," Annie said. "After a shower and change of clothes, of course."

Lenora looked down at her very dirty jeans, bits of Major's hair clinging to them and river mud and dust. In the bathroom, she looked at herself in the mirror and was shocked at what she saw: her hair was a halo of chestnut frizz and tiny bits of grass and more horse hair were interwoven with almost every strand. Yet her face looked fresh. Yes, her eyes were a little red-rimmed but she no longer had the shadow of dark circles under them. These were the eyes of a girl who was alive, she thought. She stripped out of her clothes and turned on the hot water, feeling as excited as she had ever been for indoor plumbing and lavender and coconut hair condition. After a very long and very luxurious shower, it felt so good to put on clean underwear and a flowy dress. Lenora patted her hair somewhat dry with a towel and then twisted it into a loose bun and let a few damp ringlets frame her suntanned face. She reached for her tube of mascara and then put it aside; she had not worn makeup during the last four days and Clay had seemed to like her just fine.

She walked down the stairs with her heart full of different recipes for dinner that night.

The large, ranch kitchen overlooked the barns and some of the corrals and Lenora took a moment to watch the sunset. She thought she would see Clay, but he must have been busy inside or out on the range finishing up the workday.

Lenora felt a surge of warmth pulse through her and set about paring an acorn squash to roast with pine nuts. Her aunt came back into the kitchen, as she heard the rhythmic rapping of Lenora's knife on the wooden cutting board.

"You'll not believe it, and your uncle won't admit it, but, he missed all those healthy dishes you make," Annie said. She was smiling. "And I missed you."

"I missed you, too," Lenora said and felt her eyes moisten.

The women were quiet while Lenora tossed the squash in olive oil and then spread it on a baking sheet with a few sprigs of rosemary and large wedges of tender, red onion. She pulled the oven door open and slid the tray in. They worked on a big salad with Lenora's delightfully light orange and vinegar dressing. Two large trout were wrapped in fresh lemon wedges and sage. Annie pulled a rack of fresh rolls from the bread box, and meal was complete.

As Lenora took dishes to the table she heard the men on the porch and felt her heart flutter with excitement. She turned around, and Clay was standing in the passageway watching her with his hat in his hands. His eyes were full of something she could not quite read, Lust?No, that was not it, she thought, perhaps excitement to see her.

Then her uncle and Jesse were there as well, the moment was gone as plates were filled, rolls passed and talk of the day and the trip to check on the high fences ensued. Clay sat next to her, and once their hands touched as she passed the salad dressing, and his eyes locked with hers for one, long moment. What was happening, she wondered. Was she really falling in love?

Lying in bed alone that night, she began to imagine a future at the ranch. She could see her roasted squash soup (with a garnish of pine nuts and parsley) sitting on a table surrounded by a kale and beet salad. Oh, and of course potatoes, twice baked and smothered in sharp, cheddar cheese. Would people come to the ranch for the beauty and peace? Would they come again? How she could shape life out of the hard rocks and rolling hills of this place, she wondered. But somehow, she knew that she already had all the pieces and just needed to figure out how they fit together. She sighed and rolled over in bed, it was delightful to sleep on a mattress again. Funny, how she had never realized how comfortable her bed actually was. She wondered what he was doing; in bed, or out walking the night? She pictured his shirtless body as he had stood in the creek, the early morning steam rising from the water, and the cool air all around them. The muscles in his back rippled, and she pictured her hands sliding across them.

She could not sleep, lovely mattress and fresh sheets be damned. Avoiding the creaking floorboards, she scrambled out of bed and pulled on a zip up jacket over her fitted T-shirt and boy shorts. She slipped down the stairs past her aunt and uncle's room and through the shadowy kitchen. Stepping out into the night air she felt alive. The stars were huge overhead, and her breath formed white puffs. The air had really gotten cold. She was glad to be back, but the stars and cold air made her feel so alive. Did she even want to go back east and miss the entire huge universe over her head? She realized city lights had a habit of blocking out more than just the stars at night.

Of course, he was there, over by the corrals. She leaned against the rusty rail fence next to him.

"I used to come out for a smoke. Right before I went to sleep and look over the horses," he said. "Now, I don't smoke, but the habit of checking the horses is harder to kick than the tobacco."

She glanced at him. His face was shaved smooth, though he barely grew much of a beard. The strong line of his jaw and the shadows of his eyes contrasted with the cold light from the stars. He reached for her, pulling her body to him and she was overwhelmed by his scent: alfalfa hay, honey, something minty and then a musk that made her think of wolves or mountain lions. The scent of something rugged, big, and, yes, wild.

He bent his head and kissed her. There was a neediness she had not felt out on the trail.

"Please let me make love to you?"

Her breath caught in her throat at the huskiness of his voice. His thumb caressed the inside of her thigh, sending a shiver of desire bolting through her stomach and upwards to her chest. She wondered briefly if she should try and play coy with him and make him wait. Perhaps that way he would not get bored with her. She realized all she wanted was to tumble with this man in the hay or his warm bed with soft sheets.

CHAPTER SEVEN

With her whisper of agreement, he scooped her up and carried her out of the cool night and into his bunkhouse. An old lantern-style lamp stood on a table by his bed. He set her down on a pile of warm, flannel sheets to close the door and pull off his boots. As he turned back to her and shrugged out of his coat she saw his erection already fully formed and confined by his snug jeans. Her heart kicked up the pace and her palms felt damp. *This was a man indeed!* Then he was upon her; hands roaming her body, lips kissing her ears, legs, mouth. She could barely breathe, let alone think. He was ferocious and hungry, pulling her clothes off and tasting her skin.

"You smell so good." He whispered, against her neck.

She could not reply, as he had pulled off his shirt and her shorts, and she was luxuriating in the all-encompassing feel of their skin touching. Then his pants were coming off, and she giggled to realize that he was brief-less. She held his hot and pure *man-ness* in her hands and gasped with the way she wanted nothing more than to straddle him and ride the wild ride.

He read her mind and rolled under her, while simultaneously lifting her up to settled her on his erect point.

She really gasped this time and closed her eyes as he entered her, she was all his. As her body expanded and welcomed him in, his thumb brushed against her clit which was stretched around his hard cock. Her whole body reacted to his gentle brush of fingers; she shuddered and clutched him even harder. He moaned, and she felt his desire for her to move, and so she did, riding him deeply and letting him feel her own mounting craving. He stopped her several times, his hands firm and pleading on her waist. He played with her soft skin while he brought his own fever-pitch of need back to a controllable level.

She laughed, rollicking in her power over him as he needed her and yet stopped her movement. But it was only so long that they could hold off the inevitable, and soon her need to come and his need to release were all they could feel. She pushed faster and faster over him, until she came with the intensity of a lightning rod grounding ten thousand bolts of electricity into her warm and wet body. He was eager and thrust his pelvis up as she rode downwards. He came with a loud cry, and then they were damp with sweat and lying quietly in each other's arms.

"It felt like lightning," Lenora whispered.

He laughed and pulled her so that she was nestled under his chin.

"Yeah, it kind of did," he said.

They were silent for a few minutes, and she felt herself dozing off.

"I'm not sure I've ever felt so good," Clay said. He laughed again. And her heart beat with hope.

The stars were backlit by eastern pink when she moved sleepily from the warmth of Clay's flannel sheets to her cold and rumpled bed for another hour of sleep.

After breakfast, Lenora checked her email over her second cup of chai. Suddenly, she found a building block for her new life; wellness tourism. She set down her mug and reread the email from Liz who was a head chef at a big resort. Liz served the yoga-and-tai-chi-going patrons nothing but organic fruits and vegetables and a sparse array of meats all healthfully raised and cooked.

Lenora began to ponder how a cattle ranch could transform into place where travelers from the city could find relaxation, health and peace. There were several key ingredients she knew the ranch could supply; adventure, locally raised and grown food and a beautiful destination. Yes, the ranch needed work, she could see this, but the place had good bones— no, *great* bones. Plus, with the mountains in the background and the river as well, all they really needed to do was make the ranch blend with the natural surroundings. They could use the rugged beauty of nature to highlight the weathered-chic of the buildings. Perhaps they could get rid of the old tractor skeletons in the fields, or move them so that they looked more intentional at least. All of the cows on the ranch were already grass-fed and sustainably raised. Because it was the right way to do things and so her uncle continued in that fashion and not from the new buzz around "green" and "eco-friendly." But who cares why they did it, she thought, so long as they could cash in on the craze and keep the ranch afloat.

Annie came over to the desk and touched Lenora's shoulder.

"Are you okay?" Annie said. "Your face looks odd."

"Yes. Yes, of course," Lenora replied. "Did you mean it when you and Uncle Byron said you really wanted me to stay?"

"Yes. Why what's going on? You're not ready to leave already? Oh, no did you and Clay have an argument?"

"No." Lenora blushed despite herself. "We're fine, I think."

She imagined him last night and felt her face redden further. "Aunt Annie, I'm just trying to figure out how I fit into this place."

She lifted her arms to take in the sturdy, old ranch house,

but she meant the whole west and also her life, her new life.

"So, you want to open a restaurant?" Annie said.

"Not exactly. More like a very exclusive resort," Lenora said. "I love to cook. I really do. I love to make people feel like family through food. I want it to be *good* food. Food that makes people happy and *healthy*. And, really, right now what I want to do is… you know… *in*."

"Don't say, 'dude ranch' to your uncle just yet." Annie was smiling, and her eyes were bright. She touched Lenora's hair, gently drawing the thick braid away from her niece's face.

"I think it would be good for the ranch," Annie said. "We need something new. You know we haven't increased profits in eight years? And with rising costs of feed and fuel that can only work for so long before we have to start selling things off. Like the land."

"It's just a rough plan, but I'm going to work on it," Lenora said. "Bit by bit. But for right now, I better finish up chores in the barn."

Clouds raced across a deep blue sky. Lenora took a breath of fresh, mountain air and knew that visitors to Bear Dance Ranch would love this place as much as she does. Clay came riding in on a big chestnut gelding.

"Hi," Clay said. He climbed off his horse and circled her with his arms.

He rested his chin on her shoulder, and she could smell the soap he must have used to wash up. His breath was mint and honey. She sighed and felt herself melting into the shape of his body, as his lips delicately moved from the neckline of her sweater towards her ear. He paused just where her hairline met her smooth skin, planting a trail of butterfly kisses, intense with their individual clarity.

"Want to go for a little ride this afternoon?" He said. "I'd like to take you up to Hochman's Point."

She could not help it; she turned in his arms and met his eyes, which seemed as clear and bright as before. The tiny crook of a smile in his left cheek had her heart hammering. She was speaking before she could even control herself.

"Yes, I would. Major is dying to go out for a good gallop. And I need to clear my head."

"I'll meet you in the corral after lunch?" He said.

"Yes," she said.

He bent and swiftly kissed her wind-chapped lips and left her cheeks burning with more than the brisk weather.

***

The day had turned even windier, and the horses were restless as Clay and Lenora saddled them in silence. They were out on the high ridge to the east before he spoke.

"Are you liking it here?" Clay asked.

She watched the path of a red-tailed hawk as it circled overhead, then dropped swiftly to earth somewhere ahead in the tall grasses.

"Yes. I do. I…" She said.

She paused hoping that the right words would be brought to her on the breath of cool air blowing into their faces.

"I wonder where we stand?" She said.

As soon the words left her mouth she felt regret fill her body and scrambled to fix the situation

"I mean, you know, as friends. I don't want you to feel awkward around me. I'm a big girl. I made my own choices for sure," she said.

Now she felt inane. She glanced over at him and saw him watching her, but his eyes had become guarded and she could not read them.

"You think this is a game to me?" He sounded angry.

He snatched Major's reins and tugged the horse to a standstill.

"Look, I know I'm not great at communicating all the time. I just don't want to screw up again. You're forgetting I've been married once before," Clay said.

"I've been married before, too," Lenora said. "I've picked

the wrong person as well."

The wind caught Lenora's hair, blowing loose strands across her face and making the horses' manes stream sideways.

"I just don't want you to think I'm taking this lightly, is all," Clay said.

He let go of Major's reins.

"I'm sorry," he said.

"For what?" Her voice felt a little pinched.

"For not putting this right. What I mean is… are you even staying here?" He said.

"I don't know. Maybe. Yes," Lenora said. "I'm trying to build something here, in the west."

Her heart felt light but her head was full of worries. They both stopped their horses again and looked at each other.

"I want to try and turn the ranch into a tourist retreat," she said. "We have to do something. At the rate my aunt and uncle are going, they'll have to sell the big meadow by the river at the end of the year. I think maybe, we could have a place for people to stay. I could cook their meals and then they could hike or bike or maybe even do a few trail rides."

She met his eyes squarely before she continued. He looked thoughtful.

"I think people would come here to just unwind in all this beauty. It can help people, heal them. It's been working on me. I think we could advertise that all our food comes from less than one hundred miles away and most from the ranch."

"I think it could work," he said. "I love that you want to stay. I've been so worried that you were going to go back to Chicago. And I was going to have to drive out there and convince you to come back."

Clay got off his horse and walked to Major's side. He reached up and grasped her about the waist and had her in his arms in a whirl. He kissed her hard, and she felt her body form to his. She let Major's reins slip from her fingers and instead grabbed fistfuls of his shaggy locks. *What was she coming to?* She wondered briefly as she let him slide his hand inside her jeans and stroke her back and buttocks.

"You'll come visit me tonight?" He asked.

His voice was in her ear, and his lips moved on her neck and nuzzled through her sweater to her collarbone.

"Yes," she said.

She was breathless, and the world seemed to be spinning, and she was thrilled and scared at the same time.

"I've never felt like this before. Not trying to be cliché, but really. I'm a little frightened," she said.

"That's because you hadn't met me, Baby," he said.

But he was grinning as he spoke and his eyes danced. Handsome *and* cocky male, she thought. The tension in the air eased, and she could draw deep breathe again.

She punched him in the ribs, and he squeezed her closer.

"How about a drive into the city Saturday afternoon, once I'm finished with chores? We could go see that new movie everyone is talking about, and you could help me order from a fancy restaurant all in French. Or we could go see something at the theatre?" He said

"Really? Like a date?" She said.

"Yes, like a date. Bring your toothbrush, and we can stay over somewhere," he said.

"Ok. I guess I better catch my horse." She said.

But she turned to find Major nibbling on some grass, and acting like he had not been watching the whole kissing episode.

***

There was a tiny women's boutique in town. Lenora drove in with the pretense of picking up some things for dinner. Really, her plan included lingerie. She had thrown everything even remotely lacy or sheer out after she and Mick were divorced. The only thing Clay had ever seen her in was functional cotton. She wanted something that said: *Hello!I'm falling in love with you, mister. Look at me!*

A tiny, clear bell range as she pushed open the door, and

a willowy woman looked up and smiled from her seat behind the antique cash register. She set down her novel and waved carefully manicured fingers at Lenora. The whole store smelled like rose water and something else, the beach?

"Please tell me you're looking for something wonderful?" The woman said. "Something exciting and out-of-the-ordinary."

"Well, I am. I…" Lenora said.

She paused knowing this was a small, small town, and she was new, but something in the other woman's eyes made her feel like she had found an ally.

"I'm looking for some killer lingerie!" Lenora said before she could back out.

"Yes! Finally. Do you know how hard it is to have something *unexpected* happen in this town?" The lady with the perfect nails said.

Lenora laughed and felt muscle in her neck relax. It was impossible not feel happy around this woman.

"Come to the back," the woman said.

She led Lenora through rows of bright shirts, most liberally dotted with rhinestones and glitter, to a slim section with a very nineteen-fifties looking manikin dressed in a lovely silk bustier. The delicate confection was strapless, and made of creamy colored silk with tiny, green rosebuds outlining sheer sections designed to tease the eye in a very interesting way. Lenora's stomach did a quick backflip. Clay will love this, she thought.

"Would you like to try it on?" The woman asked. And then she said, "Oh, where are my manners? I'm Rosa."

"Lenora. Yes, I would love to."

Lenora extended her hand and grasped Rosa's long, delicate fingers. She was surprised by the strength behind the woman's grip.

Lenora tried on the lovely silk and could not believe how amazing it looked against her softly glowing skin. She reached up to feel her cheeks, which were turning red just with the thought of spending time alone with Clay while she wore this scrap of clothing. The silk clung to her body, pushing her breasts together and up and wrapped her waistline and clung to her thighs as it stopped just shy of being decent.

"I'll take it," Lenora said smiling.

Rosa's deep brown eyes were huge and sparkling under her carefully applied grape eyeliner.

"Who's the lucky guy?" Rosa said.

"Clay Darkhorse. He's a cowboy who works for my aunt and uncle." Lenora said. She knew her face was still pink.

"Oh, cowboys! They're *such* bad news but so easy on the eye," Rosa said. She held up her left hand and a delicate diamond sparkled in the light. She continued, "Sometimes though, they end up being the best kind of man a girl could want."

"Really? How long have you two been together?" Lenora asked.

"Six years," Rosa said. "If you had asked me to leave sunny, California seven years ago, I would have told you to go to hell. But that cowboy of mine manages to move me here and tie me down in twenty-one days! You know he likes to brag about it. Like, you know if people ask how we met? He gets all proud and starts telling them how he moved me to the mountains!"

Lenora felt a little giddy, this woman was awesome. She realized she desperately needed a good girlfriend to hang out with on occasion.

Rosa folded the garment and put it in a beautiful purple bag. "How about lunch one day soon?" She said. "And you can tell me all about how he liked you in silk and roses?"

"Yes, sure. I'd love it really. I don't know anyone here. Sometimes it gets a little lonely," Lenora said.

"Great. Here's my card, and that's my cell number," Rosa said. "Or we could do karaoke at the Painted Pony?" She winked.

"That sounds fun! Oh, and thanks." Lenora lifted up her precious bag and smiled as she left the store.

CHAPTER EIGHT

Back at the ranch a damp wind stirred the fading leaves of the cottonwoods. Crows cawed and circled around aimlessly, as Lenora pulled up next to the barns. She felt unease set into her heart even as she reminded herself to be positive. Gathering up her bag of lingerie, she slammed the truck door behind her. Tomorrow she would be in the city with Clay; she tried to calm the anxious feeling in her stomach. Maybe she was just nervous, she thought.

It was not until sunset that the wind brought in a raven-haired girl in a jacked-up Toyota. As Lenora met her on the porch, she realized the girl was a woman, and she was Clay's ex-wife.

Of course, she would stay for dinner, Lenora thought, Clay was not yet in from the North Pasture. Lenora tried to make small talk, as she mixed pastry flour for the pot pie, all the while anxiety growing in the pit of her stomach. Crystal was beautiful.

"Where are you living now?" Lenora said.

"In Missoula. Of course. But maybe Polson soon. I can't stand the lonesome feeling of winters at these ranches. You know? Wait, you haven't been through a winter yet. Well, you'll see. It's crazy how lonely and cooped up you start feeling," Crystal said.

Lenora tried to calm herself. She glanced out the window to see Clay come cantering in on his mare, Moon. How could her aunt still be in town, she thought? Why was *she* here, and what could she possibly want from Clay, Lenora wondered.

Thankfully two trucks pulled up at that moment; one was Byron's truck, and the other belonged to the feed guy. Annie came in to help with the potatoes, and she was cordial to Crystal. Was there a secret that no one was telling her? Sometimes these ranch people were so quiet, it frightened Lenora. Would she ever learn to read between all the lines, she thought, the way they did?

As the pie baked Annie finally grasped Lenora's arm and led her down the hallway away from their visitor.

"Don't judge him too harshly," Annie said. "He was just a boy, really."

Lenora felt dread deep in her stomach. "What's going on? What happened?" Lenora said.

Annie sighed. Lenora was trying to be patient. What was going on, she felt the stab of hot anger.

"I'm only doing this," Annie said. "Because I love *both* of you."

"Clay was young. And, oh so handsome," Annie said. "And maybe a little headstrong, and the very lovely girl with black hair; who came to care for the children the next ranch over, saw him and he her, and they fell in love. Well. Well, that was Crystal. It was classic really; he got her pregnant and then they got married in a bit of a rush. It was not perfect but it worked, sort of. Clay was a good father despite his own youth. All seemed as if it was going to be fine, until the night before the child's second birthday; the baby simply died in his sleep. Crystal blamed Clay for making them live so far from the hospital."

Lenora could see Clay with a baby in his arms. She imagined the child's dark hair and large, brown eyes, just like Clay's.

"But Crystal comes back from time to time. And then

they try and make it work again," Annie said. "Clay still feels responsible is all. He can't help it. She's not always very stable, that one. She needs his help, or just to know that someone cares about her. That's all."

"I see," Lenora said.

"I'm sure this time will be different though," Annie said.

"Yes. Yes, of course."

When they returned to the kitchen the men had come in from chores, and Crystal was out with them in the big dining room. Lenora could hear Clay's voice but not what he said. Jesse came to help bring dishes out to the table and Byron was preoccupied with the feed rep, Bill Simms. Lenora carried out the hot potpie and could hardly look at Clay where he stood speaking with Crystal. She knew he looked at her and she felt like a coward when she did not meet his eyes. Instead she used the heavy pie as an excuse to look at the table. Silently, she told herself; it was a fling anyway, and if this cowboy wants to go back to his old flame, so be it.

Dinner was plated, and the feed man talked about getting them switched over to a different feed brand. Lenora kept her mouth firmly shut and would not meet Clay's eyes across the table. The only time she spoke was when Bill, the feed rep, tried to steer them away from their current horse feed.

"Why switch from a feed that works for our horses? Why should we move away from something that is more natural to what a wild horse would eat? And aids in digestion? Plus, it keeps our horses looking wonderful," Lenora said.

"I agree," Byron said.

Lenora smiled at her uncle and he nodded back, she ate the rest of her meal in silence.

After dinner Jesse and Annie were on dish duty and Lenora excused herself. She stepped out onto the porch to find Crystal and Clay standing facing each other. Clay's face was in the shadows, so Lenora could not see his eyes, but he had a hand resting on either of Crystal's shoulders. Crystal turned and looked Lenora fully in the eyes— had the two women been wild mares Crystal would have just pinned her ears at Lenora and shot out a high, hind kick.

"Is everything okay, Clay?" Lenora said. Her voice sounded high and whiny to her own ears.

"It's fine, I'll be in in just a little while, Nora," Clay said. He seemed embarrassed and did not say anything more. He looked as if his past and future were colliding and leaving him feeling out of control.

"I need to talk to my old husband about something. Go on in now," Crystal said.

Lenora backed away, turned and mumbled something before heading back into the house. Her stomach knotted around the pot pie.

She half expected Clay to be a step behind her to explain what was going on. When she realized he was not, her throat felt raw and her eyes stung. The worst part, and maybe the reason she was reacting so strongly to Crystal, was that the two of them looked so right together. Clay and Crystal looked perfectly natural and amazing standing out on the porch with the sun setting behind them. They looked like they belong on a ranch in the west. Perhaps she was jealous. Crystal was a true beauty by anyone's standards: her heavy, black hair, perfect complexion and long, long legs were only the beginning. That girl definitely did not look like she had had a baby, with her flat stomach and lean arms and thighs; she looked like a very sexy Miss Montana. Was Lenora envious of Crystal because she herself was so, so *white*, she wondered. How ironic. She instantly felt supremely bad. She had no idea the trials and tribulations Crystal, or her forbearers, might have gone through at the hands of her own, white ancestors. She really felt like a good cry in Major's mane was what she needed. The way she felt left her feeling too angry and confused. But she was scared of what she might find on the front porch. She went into the bathroom and took a quick, hot shower. Resting her head against the glass door she remembered *the dark time* and realized she could get through this. Overall, she was a pretty, mature women; even though she felt fifteen years old again and jealous as hell right at the moment. She would grow through this and one day look back and smile. The very thought of looking back made her cry a few tears, which scalded her cheeks more than the steaming shower. She really wished she could go see her horse. Since she could not, she put lavender lotion on her legs and pulled on a form fitting, black dress.

As Lenora checked her email, she realized a trip back to Chicago was coming up on Sunday. She could take care of the last medical bills and catch up with Liz and the other girls from the barn. Overall, she realized she needed more girl time. What about the lady from the cute boutique? On a whim, she rummaged through her purse and found the card with Rosa's cell number scrawled across it in purple pen. Without giving herself time to think she dialed the number.

"Hi there," Rosa said.

She sounded as if she knew exactly who it was on the other line.

Lenora laughed despite herself: "Hi. This is the crazy girl, who bought that lingerie from you?"

"Well, I'm so glad you called," Rosa said. "I could use a drink and tonight seems the perfect night for doing just that. I bet you have a story about a good-looking cowboy to tell me."

"I do." Lenora said.

"The Painted Pony?" Rosa said.

"Yes, of course," Lenora said. "Give me twenty minutes."

The bar was quiet; a few regulars sat on stools facing the polished mirrors, and two men played a game of pool under the hand-hewn beams holding the place up. Over by the jukebox, a man nursed a drink and an album of some sort. Lenora felt like she had stepped into some kind of eighties movie but could not back out now. She sat at a sunken booth and waited only a moment for the bartender to bring her a cold Corona.

Rosa entered the bar with a flourish of turquoise scarf

and tall boots.

"Two shots of tequila, Timmy," She called to the bartender and sat down across from Lenora. "So, did he like the silk?" Rosa said.

"I don't know," Lenora said.

"So, what's the problem?" Rosa said.

"His *ex* is back," Lenora said.

"Oh, crap. Tim! Another round, pronto!" Rosa said.

The first round had not yet arrived.

"That little, black-haired thing doesn't have a hold on him except in the past. One thing I've learned about living here; is these people don't let the past go easy. But, but when they do, it's for good. Don't give up. Do you hear me? This is hard country stuck between the mountains the way it is," Rosa said. "He'll come to his senses in no time, I'll bet."

Two empty shot glasses a piece sat on the table between them. Lenora felt dizzy. Someone had put an old Patsy Kline song on the jukebox.

"The mountains breed very stubborn, and, if I may say so, not always the brightest people." Rosa ran her hand through her black curls. "Nevertheless," she continued. "You have your heart on a cowboy, so we had better figure out what's going on in that thick skull of Clay's. But, in the meantime, let's get drunk and sing some karaoke."

Lenora laughed and downed her third tequila; suddenly the world did not seem so cold and uncaring anymore.

Five, or maybe seven, shots later, the Dixie Chicks', "Wide Open Spaces" played on the karaoke machine, and the door to the bar banged open. Clay with rain-jeweled hair and a heavy coat walked in. Lenora felt a thrill of joy to see him, even in her inebriated state, and smiled to herself but kept up the beat with Rosa; who it turned out could really sing, tequila or no. Quite a crowd had gathered at The Painted Pony, once word of two drunk girls singing about cowboys went around the town. A group of rowdy men were drinking hard, and singing along as well. In general, it was the most fun Lenora had had in a very long time.

She watched Clay warily as he ordered a beer and sat at the bar with the others. Lenora decided to ignore him and continue with the song.

Somewhere after, "Before He Cheats," and maybe her eighth shot, Lenora had to take a break. She and Rosa stepped outside into the chill rain, the air felt wonderful on Lenora's hot face. Headlights pulled into the parking lot, and a tall cowboy got out of a dually truck and headed towards them.

"Uh-oh. I've been found," Rosa said.

"What the hell, Darling?" The tall man said.

"Just having a little fun on a miserable night!" Rosa said.

"I can tell," he said.

Just then the door to the bar opened, spilling golden light across the gravel parking lot, and Clay emerged. He was gentle as he took Lenora's elbow.

"Can we talk?" Clay said. He turned to Rosa's husband, a smile quick and full of white teeth spread across his face.

"Hi Landon. Nothing like these gals, really, is there?" Clay said.

"I think you've found one as feisty as my Rosie," Landon said. He pulled his wife close enough to plant a swift kiss on her perfectly made-up lips.

Lenora did not know exactly whom Clay meant, but imagined it was she and Rosa to which he was referring. In her drunken state she had no idea if his observation was a compliment or an insult. Lenora was feeling distinctly dizzy, now that they were outside and away from the music and bright lights.

"Sure, why would there be anyone else like us?" Lenora said. Knowing full well her tone was dripping with sarcasm, she wished she could stop, but her tongue and lips moved all on their own.

"You want to tell me why your ex-wife is back?" Lenora said. "Why you're touching her like that? The wife you had a baby with and never even told me about? Why didn't you tell me your baby died?"

Something in her drink-sodden mind realized what she had just said, a second before Clay's eyes became very sad, and then his face went blank. Lenora felt like she was on a bucking horse; her world was tilting and she was going to hit the ground hard but the ride had started; or in this case the words had left her mouth, and there was no going back. She would just have to try and land as well as she could and then access the damage when her head was clear.

"I'm driving you back to the ranch. C'mon," Clay said.

Rosa quickly wrapped her arms around Lenora. "It's okay," she whispered. "The two of you just need to talk your way through this."

Rosa released her, and Clay headed towards his truck. Lenora followed, wishing she was not drunk and sad.

"I'm sorry. I didn't mean it like that. I, I just want to…I just wanted to understand," Lenora said.

But the damage was done. Clay barely looked back as Lenora followed.

"I didn't think the right time had come… for me to tell you," Clay said.

"Really?" Lenora said. "How intimate do we have to get? For you to let me into your head and heart a little?"

"I thought I told you everything you needed to know," Clay said.

"Really? I told you everything about my asshole ex, about my mom dying. I told you about lying on the bathroom floor and not wanting to ever get up again," Lenora said. "I bared my soul to you."

"I know you did," Clay said.

He helped her into the truck. She wanted to reach out and grab him and feel him hold her. Obviously, the past still hurt him, he seemed so distant. He climbed in and started the engine. The vinyl seats were cold against her legs. She rested her head on the window and tried to calm her rapidly beating heart. Suddenly, in less than six hours, her new love had fallen to pieces around her. She slumped against the passenger door as they drove home in silence.

CHAPTER NINE

He must have helped her to her bed, because when she finally woke, with a soggy feeling in her head and unease in her stomach, she had slept through chores and breakfast. Her aunt was sitting beside her bed with a cup of peppermint tea.

"How do you feel?" Annie asked.

"Like I drank too much tequila," Lenora answered.

"Well, best to just take today as a sick day and lay in bed," Annie said.

"Oh, Aunt Annie is she gone?"

"Yes, she left this morning after breakfast."

"What did she want?"

"The same as always; a little money and a safe place to spend the night." Annie said. "He used to go back to her. You know? She'd stay for a week or two and they'd seem pretty happy, but then something always made them fight, and she'd leave again. He'd be moody for a month and then get over it and try and date some girl from another town. He's a good man, Lenora, but he has a past just like everyone does."

Annie looked at her hands before meeting Lenora's eyes; the expression in the older woman's eyes reminded her of

Maura, her mother. She wondered if her aunt was upset with the way she had acted last night, disappointed even. Lenora felt more embarrassed as she remembered her cold words to Clay. The drinking and singing had been fun, but her extreme reaction to Crystal's arrival at the ranch was disturbing.

Lenora was silent as she sat up in bed and sipped the tea, her mind flitting from fear to fear like a bird trapped in a glass house. The last year seemed so long and heavy. How could she really go through anymore sadness? She had thought this would be a fun roll in the hay and a simple romance, but she was beginning to wonder if such a thing even existed. Who in this world did not have baggage and sadness and loss weighing them down? Not she, and apparently not Clay either, she realized.

"I just wish that he would have told me about the baby," Lenora said. "And a little more about Crystal too. I mean, I was grieving Mom so hard. I could have understood his pain."

"I don't know what to say. He should have told you," Annie said. "I think he's just a product of his upbringing. Have you noticed how he always wants to take care of everything? How he's always acting like he has it under control?"

"Yes," Lenora said. "Even last night, when he was really pissed off at me he still helped me into the truck. He was even polite."

Annie sighed. "Did you at least have a good time?"

"Yeah. I sang karaoke."

"So I heard. Get some rest today," Annie said. She gave Lenora a soft smile before closing the door.

Lenora slept until afternoon, and then crept downstairs and out the back door. She bridled Major and slipped out of the barnyard and into the hills. The day was cloudy; overhead gray shapes shifted and twisted moving steadily east. She let Major pick the direction, and he went east towards the crown of hills topped with a few pines. She let him climb steadily, his huge Arabian lungs filling with clean, mountain air. Bareback under her, she could feel the long dorsal muscles along his spin and the strength from his hindquarters. His velvety coat was warm through her jeans, and she leaned forward and buried her hands and face in his thick mane. They stopped at the top of the hill. Below them the ranch consisted of tiny dot buildings and outlines of fencing. She slid off Major and let him eat the thick, green grass underneath an old cedar tree. She sat on a stone and stared off to the north where the real peaks began, and felt the first hot gulp of sadness well up in her throat and then drip down her cheek. Alone, with only her horse as witness she sunk down into a deep pit of self-pity. Why so many bad things? Why so many lost people in her life, she wondered. She imagined telling her mom about Clay and last night; then she really cried.

***

When Lenora came in for the dinner, she found Clay's place at the table empty

"Clay will be back by Monday," Byron said. "He went on up to the North Pasture to check on the herd."

"Ok, I understand," Lenora said.

She ducked her head so that her eyes could not give away her hurt. How could he leave, when they needed to talk about what had happened last night, she wondered. She knew she should have gone to find him when she woke that morning, but she had needed some space to understand her own reaction. To have him leave the ranch and not talk to her seemed like a huge betrayal of trust.

"I actually go back east on Sunday. To, to go visit some friends from home," she continued: "Just for a few days."

The look of fear on her aunt's face was clear, even her uncle looked surprised.

"But you're coming back, right?" Annie said.

"Yes, of course." Lenora said. "I've planned this trip for

months. It has nothing to do with Clay."

But she wondered how awkward it would be to see Clay every day, be close to him and for the memory of their shared nights to lie between them like unpicked fruit left to spoil. Why had she ever started a fling with a cowboy, she wondered, and a cowboy that worked for her aunt and uncle. What must they think of her, showing up here and getting swept off her feet and into Clay's arms?

"Well, I'll drive you to the airport," Annie said.

After dinner, as Lenora helped clear the dishes Her uncle put his hand on her shoulder and spoke softly, "Come back to us, now you hear? You know we've all grown really fond of your blueberry crisp." Byron winked and Lenora felt a little less restricted in her breathing. A trip back home would be good; perhaps it would even lend new perspective to her life in Montana.

***

On the car ride to the airport, the clear sky promised a beautiful day.

"I'm going to miss you. It's really just a few days, right?" Annie said.

"Yes, I'm coming back," Lenora answered.

She was resolute with her tone, but in the back of her mind she wondered if it would be easier to just stay in Chicago? She knew she could not run forever, she would have to face Clay again. Embarrassment and anger were a deadly mix, and both boiled in her stomach just thinking about Clay and his ex-wife standing on the porch. Why had she not known what to say at that awkward moment?

"I feel silly for falling for him, Aunt Annie," Lenora said.

"Oh, Dear. Don't. It will all work out. I'm sure you two just need to have some time to breath. It's been quite hot and heavy between you two hasn't it? Sometimes a little time away makes it easier to clear the head."

"I should have never slept with your Ranch Foreman,

though. I'm sorry. I feel so silly. Like a little girl. I just... I just hadn't felt good in so long and he made me feel so *alive*."

Lenora was gushing now, the words falling from her mouth with regret. These were things she would have told her mother. How life marched forward despite loss, death, love.

"Darling," Annie said. She placed her hand on Lenora's cheek even as she drove the truck down the winding, mountain highway. "I don't think it's *just* sex with you and Clay? Do you? I see something more in both of your faces, when you look at each other."

Lenora was silent thinking this over and watching the mountains give way to city and the hustle and bustle, which she realized she did not miss. At the airport, before getting out of the truck, Lenora hugged Annie.

"I think that's what I'm so scared of, Aunt Annie. I'm scared that there is more between Clay and me. I'm not ready for *more*. I feel like I'm raw from Mom. And from Mick, and I don't know if I have any love left to give! I feel used up. By, by life I guess. I feel used up by life."

"I know you do but you can't give up because you've had a bad run. That's not how life works." Annie squeezed Lenora's hand. "Be safe and come back to us."

Lenora walked to her boarding gate, her mind whirling with a thousand emotions as she headed back to her old life.

***

It was afternoon when Lenora landed in Chicago. She gathered her bags and headed out into the rush of noise and traffic to look for her friend. Standing next to her car at the busy airport pick up terminal, Liz was a chic, Chicagoan with square bangs, wide rimmed, black glasses as well as designer leggings and heels.

"You're here!" Welcome home," Liz said.

The city no longer felt like home, but Lenora would not say so to her friend. Had the sky always been so close and gray? She watched the hurrying people around her with their tired faces. Her head felt thick and her movements slow and awkward as everyone rushed around her. Why were all these people in such a hurry, she wondered. Their movements seemed inefficient and the air smelled like exhaust fumes.

"Thank you so much for picking me up. It's so nice to be back to see you," Lenora said.

"Of course! I've seriously missed you. Plus, you keep hinting at some hottie who works for your aunt and uncle, and I *really* want to hear all about him," Liz said. "The guys in this city just plain suck. Is he a cowboy? Can he, like, rope horses and ride wild mustangs and stuff?"

"His name is Clay. And I'm not sure we are going to work out. I'm still getting over my divorce and he's got an ex-wife and all the baggage that comes with that," Lenora said.

"Oh, I see. Well, at least you have a guy even if you aren't quite ready for him. I swear every other guy I meet is a stockbroker. They have no imagination, and I really don't want to hear how they single handedly are going to get our economic growth back to 10 percent!" Liz said. "Now, let's get you out to the horse barn to see everyone, then a late lunch."

It was good to see Liz, even if the city seemed rushed and dirty. They loaded her one suitcase into Liz's hatchback and pulled onto the freeway heading towards the suburbs on the southwest side of Chicago.

The day slipped away, filled with seeing new horses at the barn where Lenora had boarded Major and all of her old riding friends. Oddly enough, the people and places of her previous life no longer felt as if they belonged to her. Something had changed, and all through the day Lenora tried to put her finger on it. Late in the evening, tucked into Liz's spare room, she realized she had transformed into a different person than the girl who lost her mother and broke into a million pieces. Her mother's death had been the beginning of a huge shift in her life. She thought back over the two years and realized that all she had been trying to do was to close the old doors in her life with grace and open the new ones with courage. Thinking of new doors, she wondered what Clay was doing? Had he made it safely back from the summer pasture? What would it be like at the ranch if the two of them had to avoid each other? Should she try and move into town when she went back west? She realized suddenly that no matter what happened with her and Clay, she would stay in Montana. The big sky and open space of that place had awakened more life in her than she had ever thought she could experience. Her home was no longer in Chicago. That was at least comforting to know where she belonged even if she did not yet know with whom. Maybe she was just fine by herself, and she knew that was the truth of the matter; she could be very happy and fulfilled all by herself. What she did need was the blossoming relationship with her Aunt and Uncle and Rosa. The thought of Rosa made her smile. She hoped her friend and her hunk of a husband had enjoyed some great makeup sex.

Her whole vacation would have been relaxing and wonderful except she ran into Mick. Or, she suspected, he came to find her. Who had told him she was back? Not Liz, one of the girls from the café where they had dinner, perhaps. She really had no idea but wished they had not meddled in her life.

"Why didn't you tell me you were coming back?" Mick said.

He stood in the doorway to the tack room. Liz had dropped Lenora off at the horse barn so that she could ride and hang out with the barn manager, Francine. How typical of Mick, Lenora thought, to be angry about some perceived slight.

"I had no reason to tell you, Mick," Lenora said.

She was trying her best not to look directly at him; he was dressed in tailored pants and had a heck of a tan. She knew most women found him to be a very attractive man. Once upon a time Lenora would have agreed.

The problem had always been that he was too good

looking and very charming. He would come across as the nicest guy in the world really, and maybe he was, especially if you were a girl. Mick loved women; simply no way around that fact, she thought. Sometimes, as Lenora had learned, several at one time.

"Well, I assumed we were still friends," Mick said.

He looked like some kind of GQ model with his stubble and cautiously, messy dark hair. Lenora found herself picturing Clay. He had mud on his boots, hair shaggy around his collar and his eyes so full of joy as he smiled at her on the first morning after they had made love.

"I have nothing to say to you," Lenora said. "I can't believe you would even come here."

"Wait, wait," he said. "I was hoping you would have dinner with me. I really owe you a nice meal and an apology."

"We aren't friends, Mick. And I have no desire to waste my time being around you, or listening to your excuses anymore," Lenora said. "Now, go live your life, as I am doing just that for myself. I have no more time for you."

Wow, that felt good, she thought and turned and walked into the barn, slipping into a stall with a large warmblood horse. She sighed; it had perhaps not been the best idea to picture Clay on that morning, not so very long ago, but it had given her strength. Damn, he had looked amazing, she thought. The perfect amount of skin showing through the V of his shirt had been alluring. His pure black hair still dripping from the icy mountain stream. And his eyes, she could only describe them as rich as the landscape and his own heritage in that wild place. They were so clear, so bright, a gift from God to remind him of his deep roots, surely? Clay had made her brave; the mountains had lent her confidence. Suddenly, after borrowing the gifts, she realized they were now hers. No longer would she give into her womanizing, ex-husband.

Lenora admired the people she was meeting in the west; they would not start trouble, but if they had to, they would finish it quickly and with the confidence that they were in the right. Oh, why was she here, she wondered, in Chicago. Suddenly, she was ready to be on the plane and headed west. She would take Major out on an early morning gallop and leave tracks in the frost blanketing the hills. Together they would greet the sunrise and feel the quiver of life as it pulsed through the world. She was ready to go home.

***

The next day as she hugged Liz goodbye she felt sad. Perhaps sensing this, Liz hugged tighter.

"I'll try and come out to visit for Christmas," Liz said. "I always have some time off for the holidays, and I'm sure the ranch is beautiful in winter."

"Oh, please do!" Lenora said. She felt herself smile.

On the plane she sat next to a lovely lady who spoke of going to visit her granddaughters. As they landed in Denver, because nonstop flights to Montana from Chicago were not an option, a huge bolt of lightning touched down next to their plane. All the lights at the terminals flickered. The passengers were ordered briskly off the plane. Her flight to Montana was delayed, indefinitely. Using her cell phone, she called the ranch and left a message for her aunt, forewarning her to not come to the airport.

Lenora leaned against the window and watched lightning play across the sky. Of course, her mind was reliving a different storm, one where she was wrapped in the arms of the sexiest, kindest man she had ever known.

"He must be something special to have you looking so sad," said a voice from behind her.

Lenora turned and found a small woman sitting on the ground beside the long row of windows. The woman was surrounded by bags made of brightly colored cloth. Her hair was white and very long, bordering her face which was the color of the inside of a walnut shell.

"Sit. Eat with me. You can tell me all about this young

brave of yours," she said.

Lenora sat down. She wondered how this woman had known she loved a Native American man. Did it matter? The old woman handed Lenora a Tupperware bowl with succotash in it; a mixture of beans, rice, corn, onions and tomatoes. With no fork appearing, Lenora dipped her fingers into the bowl. The food was amazing.

"What's in this?" Lenora said. "I'm sorry. I'm tired and have no manners. I'm Lenora."

"Susan," the old woman said. "Sometimes they, my family, call me Black-Eyed Susan. Like the flowers. You know?"

"Yes. Yes, I do know," Lenora said. "Where are you going from here?"

"New Mexico. Home," Susan said. "You know all you have to do is take him back. If you want him, of course."

Susan looked at Lenora and she realized the woman's eyes were indeed black. A shiver ran down her spine. This perfect stranger looked at her as if she knew every thought in Lenora's head and emotion in her heart.

"Go to the mountains, the desert, the lake. Go wherever you can to be alone, and then ask," Susan said. "You ask *La Que Saba*, she is the one who knows all about women, and woman trouble. You ask her to help you. But make sure, Young One, that you want, really want what you ask for. Because she will give him to you. Is this man the one you want?"

"I, I don't know. That's the trouble. I'm so unsure of myself right now," Lenora said. "My mother is dead."

She had no idea why she was telling this strange old lady about her mother. Nor, why she was starting to cry. She set down the bowl of succotash and wiped at her face. The late hour, and being in an airport for so long must be making her crazy, she had never liked the harsh glare of the LED lights and long corridors of these places. Outside the storm raged on, lashing the terminal windows with rain and then lighting the runways, filled with grounded planes, in eerie brilliance.

"I'm embarrassed how I acted around his ex-wife," Lenora said. "And by how I over-reacted with him. And, well with the whole situation really. I'm not sure why I'm so freaked out by everything."

There, she had said it. Was it because of Mick and his cheating, betrayal of their marriage or the loss of her mother? No, it was more than that, she had lost trust in her own judgement, she doubted her mind, heart and gut and found herself adrift with no guide and so many worries. Lenora looked down at her hands.

Susan peeled the shiny wrapper from a thick, chocolate bar and smacked her lips as she broke off the first piece, popping it in her mouth. Lenora watched the old woman, irritated with herself for spilling so much of her heart into a conversation with a stranger. For all she knew Susan might be a homeless woman, or maybe mentally ill.

Breaking off a huge wedge of chocolate, Susan handed it over to Lenora, and kept offering the piece until she realized refusing was not only rude but futile. It really did taste amazing, nutty and richer than American chocolate. Lenora nibbled her wedge in silence, feeling more and more sorry for herself. Why did she pick the complicated guys, she wondered? Why did Clay have to be so damn nice to Crystal? Did he not see how insecure she had felt? Why could he not just cut ties with the past and only do things that would make her feel safe and loved? Wow, she stopped the litany in her head just long enough to realize her mind was speaking self-absorbed crazy talk.

"Maybe," Lenora said. "I'm not quite ready for a man in my life?"

Susan looked up from her chocolate wedge, her lips and teeth stained brown.

"Ahh, so you do want him! You know. He knows. But you don't want to scare him off with your needs, do you?" Susan said.

"I'm just not sure I'm ready to be in a relationship that's so serious. My marriage ended just a little over a year ago.

And then. And then, my mom died," Lenora said.

"Sing her praises and marry the brave. Have ten little babies to commemorate your mother," the old women said. She shrugged her shoulders and Lenora realized how tiny she was under her layers of shawls.

"You make everything so hard," Susan said. "So many decisions. Go to the mountains, ask, listen, act. That's it! Why so much thinking?"

She pointed to her head and then made circles with her finger to illustrate her theory that Lenora was thinking too much, all the time grinning with her chocolate colored teeth. Lenora smiled as well. Really, it was impossible not to like the crazy, old woman. Pulling her carry-on bag closer, she leaned against the wall of windows next to Susan.

The announcer was reading off her flight numbers. Lenora opened her eyes and was greeted by the harsh light of the terminal as well as the first silver, gray of dawn. Glancing out the windows, she realized the storm was over and the runways full of departing planes. Next to her the floor was empty, Susan was gone. Lenora rubbed her eyes amazed that she had fallen asleep in the crowded waiting area with so many sounds and lights. Where, she wondered, could the old lady have gone? Had she dreamt her? Lenora stood as passengers began to line up to board the plane. She looked everywhere. Maybe she had imagined the whole thing. As she fished in her purse for her boarding pass Lenora looked at her hand and realized it was stained with rich, dark chocolate.

CHAPTER TEN

He was waiting for her at the baggage claim. His hands were shoved in his jeans pockets, and he had his hat hooked on his thumb. It was the most awkward Lenora had ever seen him, and yet he looked more sexy and gorgeous to her than ever before. He saw her walking towards him, and gave her his half smile making her heart lurch with the violence of a colt just out of the bucking chute. She realized, as she got closer, his eyes were guarded. She wondered what he had come to say to her.

When she reached him, he had already found her bag, then he led the way through the crowded airport.

As they stepped outside he turned to her. "How was your trip?"

"It was really good. So nice to see all my old friends."

She had no idea what else to say. Small talk was not her strength, and certainly not Clay's either.

They were both silent as they walked across the sky bridge, and into the parking garage. He held the door to his truck for her and she slid inside and felt the familiar cracked, vinyl bench seat. He got behind the wheel and carefully maneuvered the truck out of the busy garage and onto the freeway. It was not until they left the city behind that he spoke.

"I should have told you about my son. I should have told you more about Crystal."

"I don't know what to say… why? Why didn't you?"

"I guess," he paused. "I guess I thought it would be bad luck."

"What?" Lenora said. She was getting mad.

"Bad luck? Well, I'll tell you what is bad luck; to have your ex-wife show up when your new girlfriend is making dinner! Or, if I'm not your girlfriend, then your little friend-with-benefits, or whatever the hell I am!" She forced herself to lower her voice. She was not sure exactly why she was mad. Maybe it had something to do with feeling very vulnerable. She would have stayed mad, but somehow the tears started to come. Clay was already pulling the truck off the freeway. He did not say anything until they turned down a dirt road, and the hills silently welcomed them. Lenora faced away from him, looking out the window and willing herself to stop. She did not want his pity. As silly, and completely unattainable, as it was, she wished that she had met Clay before she had married Mick. She wished, for that long and painful moment, that she could have been Clay's first wife. Even while she logically knew how silly and destructive this thought was, she could not shake it from her mind. Perhaps she was overcompensating due to seeing Mick over the weekend. For so long she had been more hurt than angry, and now here was anger. Anger over her poor choices, and now she was blaming Clay for his choices. She wiped at her eyes, embarrassed by her thoughts and thankful he could not see inside her head.

"Please look at it from my point of view," Clay begged.

Lenora was not really listening. She felt him slide across the seat and pull her around to face him. He smoothed the hair back from her face, but she did not look up to meet his eyes.

"I'm sorry I didn't tell you. I'm just as scared of this as you are. I've lost people, too, don't you see? I didn't know what to do that night at the bar. You were acting so angry," he said.

He ran his hands down her back, across her shoulders. It felt so good for him to touch her, she thought.

"I'm sorry I got so mad," Lenora said.

She knew her face was a mess; she had put makeup on for the airport. He put his thumb under her chin, and gently lifted. She met his eyes and saw that he looked tired. Heavy lines framed his mouth.

"Lenora, I don't know how to tell Crystal 'no' when she comes around asking for help, she's still hurting from the baby and our divorce," Clay said. "I just feel like it's my duty to help her, if I can. You should know though, I don't want her anymore as my lover. We haven't been like that in a long while."

He took a deep breath and kissed her forehead.

"Also, you and me aren't just 'friends-with-benefits.' How can you say that?" Clay's eyes were deep brown and his voice low.

"I don't want to get hurt," Lenora said. "I'm finally feeling like I might live again. And then I meet you and it's all this raw emotion all over. I just want to be okay."

"You think I want to get hurt?" Clay said. "I don't need that any more than you do. You can waltz onto the ranch, and then out as you please. I've made a promise to your uncle, and I intend to keep it."

Lenora looked up at him and saw that he spoke the truth. His eyes looked vulnerable.

"What promise did you make my uncle?" She asked.

"That I'd stick around and help him. That I wouldn't go off rodeoing and chasing girls," Clay said. "When I was younger all I wanted to do was to go rodeo. And I did, a lot. But when I started working for your uncle, he helped me with so many things. You know? Kind of looked after me. Hell, Annie stitched me up after this one event where that damn steer broke my rib and sliced down my side. You know the scar."

She did. She could remember seeing it flicker white across his ribs in the light of the fire, on their first night in the mountains.

She breathed in the scent of him: leather, mint and honey.

"Are you coming back to pack?" He asked.

"No, I'm coming back to stay. I decided that a few days into my trip. No matter what happens," Lenora said.

"Good," Clay responded

"I want us to be friends," Lenora said. "Clay, I want us to be able to work together. Do you really feel okay about me trying to do the guest ranch thing?"

"We have to save the ranch," he said. "I'm okay with it. Just none of that stupid, city slickers stuff."

"How about the Nature Conservancy?" She said.

"Yes, I'm good with all of it. *Really.*" Clay said.

He looked right at her. She thought he could read all her tumbling emotions in her eyes, and so she glanced away—putting distance between them without moving an inch. It was now or never, she realized.

"I think we should be *only* friends," She said.

She had imagined this moment all the way back on the plane. Just thinking about being so close to him every day and yet not being able to reach out and touch him made her feel cold inside. What if their hands were to brush as they passed a bridle for a horse or a plate at dinner? What would she tell her troubled heart, as it lurched to life only to be stalled by her resolute mind? She did not know, but she did know that she wanted this new family she had found. She wanted it with her whole being and Clay was part of that family, and she would not lose him, nor all the rest of it due to silly lust. She had been lonely; he had been lonely. They had found each other in their time of need. But really, when it came right down to it, she would rather be his friend and business partner forever than lose him due to a few nights of hot sex.

"Friends?" He said, pulling her out of her reverie. He looked stunned. "I would rather not lose you or my new family because of sex," she said.

"You don't have to lose anything," he said. "Just stay. Don't leave the ranch."

"I'm not. I told you. But I want us to be able to work together. I need you, Clay," Lenora said. Her heart was pounding, so she hurried on. "To make this whole ranch transformation happen."

"Friends, huh?" He said. He was looking at his hands. It was hard to swallow.

"Look, I want to make this work," she said. "Okay? I want all of us to be able to live together. I'm sorry it ever went so far."

"Really? You're sorry?" Clay said. He reached up and ran his hands through his hair.

"I think you're overreacting," Clay said. "We're good for each other. Can't you see that?"

Lenora bit her lip, hard. Now was not the time to go soft and let him know that she had her own doubts. She had to look out the window; she was so far from sorry. She would treasure those nights in the mountains forever. He was putting the truck in gear and pulling onto the highway. She carefully kept her eyes on the window, trying to only see the beauty of the wild countryside as they ascended the mountain road. He did not say anything else the rest of the ride home. Carefully, furtively she glanced at him from the corner of her eye; his jaw was clenched and worked from side to side. When they stopped in front of the ranch house he turned to her, his eyes full of questions

"Are you sure?" Clay said. His lips clamped around the words as they left his mouth.

"Yes," she said.

"Please look me in the eyes, Lenora."

She did, unsure if he could see past her determination to make it all work out. She wondered if he could see all the way to where her deep sadness lay like a pool of still water.

His eyes were so intense that she felt dizzy for a moment. She had to look away, and when she glanced out the windshield of the truck she saw the first snowflakes begin to fall. Winter was coming.

"Ok. I guess this is how you want it," Clay said.

"Thanks for the ride," Lenora said. She felt ridiculous but did not know what else to say. Part of her desperately wanted to prolong their time alone in the isolation of the truck.

"Yeah, sure," Clay said.

He moved first and was out of the truck with the grace and ease of movement she so admired. His back was straight as he walked away to the barns and fields and open spaces she knew he loved. Annie came out on the porch wearing a heavy cardigan. Lenora quickly swallowed the lump in her throat and grabbed her bag before stepping out to hug her aunt.

"Oh, I missed you!" Annie said.

"Me too. I'm back, though. And we have a few months to get this guest ranch going," Lenora said.

"Oh, good! So, you really are staying?" Annie said.

"Yes. Everyone keeps asking that," Lenora said.

"What about you and Clay? Oh, wait come inside. I'm being too nosey, and it's cold out here," Annie said.

"We are good friends," Lenora said. "That's what's best for both of us really."

Annie held the door, and Lenora felt a great sense of home as she walked into the ranch house. A fire was burning in the great hearth, and she could smell spiced apple cider. Suzie came over to sniff her bags, and to be scratched behind the ears.

"You and Clay decided this?" Annie said.

"Yeah, we did," Lenora said.

"Ok, then." Annie gave her a piercing look but said no more.

Her aunt poured hot cider while Lenora went to her room and changed into some comfortable pants and an oversized sweater. She felt tired and wanted to lie down, but knew her aunt would want to hear about her trip and she could use the distraction. Thinking about Clay and her own iron-willed decision right now might lead her to second guess herself and go running out to find her cowboy and plead with him to please love her forever. No reason to dwell in her own thoughts tonight.

CHAPTER ELEVEN

Winter came. Clay was icy polite and avoided her for most of the late fall and even into December, but then he relented, a little. The whole ranch crew was busy emptying out the old calving shed and turning it into an indoor arena, as well as putting new drywall in the ancient but structurally-sound bunkhouses. The indoor arena was a much needed tool which would enable Clay to take on more training horses during the long, snow-filled months.

Lenora's plan revolved around turning the two bunkhouses into swanky private quarters for guests. Each room would have massive beds, antique light fixtures, lush sheepskin rugs, and fireplaces. The highlight of each bunkhouse was windows overlooking the beautiful pastures. The bunkhouses were the perfect buildings to convert into guest quarters since they sat far away from the main barns and the ranch house. The buildings were partially hidden by a small rise.

***

One evening Lenora went to secretly watch Clay start the three year old horses under saddle. She was lurking in the barn next to the arena. It was just a week before Christmas, and she shivered in the lightly falling snow.

"I know you're there," Clay said. "So you might as well come out."

She felt silly as she stepped into the arena. He sat on a lovely gray filly that had a future in the show ring.

"The lady who owns her is looking to turn this girl into a show jumper," Clay said. "And I don't know the first thing about that. You want to ride her?"

"Yes, I would," Lenora said.

He dismounted gracefully. He wore a fleece hat and thick flannel shirt, and he looked tired.

Their hands brushed as he handed her the reins, but she was almost immune to the electricity she still felt.

"She's sensitive. Don't rush her," Clay instructed

Lenora liked the way the filly felt beneath her. She asked the horse to trot. The little horse accepted the bit graciously and was quick to move off of Lenora's leg as well. She eased the mare into a canter and felt herself smile at the eagerness of the horse to comply. After a few circles and changes of direction they came to a stop in front of Clay.

"Can we put my saddle on her next time?" Lenora said. "And maybe set up a few poles for her to trot over?"

"You going to help me with her?" he said.

"Yes. If you'll let me," Lenora replied.

He kicked the sand footing in the arena before looking up at Lenora where she sat on the gray mare. His face was guarded but his eyes soft.

Over the course of the next week Lenora helped Clay with the filly. She found herself watching him on the horses hungrily; there was no other way to explain it. He was graceful on their backs and gentle on the ground, never losing his patients when they were difficult to handle and argued with his every request.

Lenora began to get the idea that he had moved on. Of course, he was polite, kind, even gentle with her. Yet some of the passion she had felt between them seemed to have melted away. This put a sliver of ice through her heart, but it also gave her some small comfort. All was becoming right and sane in her world again. She could deal with her own ragged emotions, but seeing him angry and hurt had made her own pain so much worse. Plus, with all that needed to be done to get the ranch ready for the first guests, she really had no time to spare. She had to force herself to take time out to enjoy the mountains and get Major the exercise he needed. She assured herself that she had made the right decision on their drive home from airport.

One morning as she came in from a brisk canter on her horse, she noticed a shiny dually and horse trailer in the drive. She heard Clay in the arena, and when she glanced inside he was showing a lovely blond woman the gray filly. Lenora untacked Major and curried out the saddle marks, all the while watching the blond faun all over Clay. What woman would not, she reasoned. He looked the part with his worn jeans covered by tan chaps, thick jacket, scuffed boots and carefully tied wild rag. His intense, sexy eyes were the final touch.

Major brought her back from her angry spying with a sharp swish of his tail.

"Sorry boy," Lenora said. She realized too late that she had been applying all her pent-up fervor to brushing his side.

Thankfully, the full-figured blonde was climbing into her truck. Lenora found herself looking down at her own body. What had Clay even seen in her anyway? Considering how jealous she was because a woman was simply talking to Clay, it was probably better that they just stayed friends. This way was best; she could stay at the ranch and have a family and home. But her mind kept bringing up the image of Clay that night in the cave. She saw him gently peeling her out of her wet clothes and then kissing her, his hands running the length of her body. She shivered, the memory so intense that she felt her whole body ache to be next to him. She wanted to feel his skin on hers. She realized she had to stop the thought. Perhaps one day she would be able to control these feelings and see him as a very good friend. She loved working the horses with him; in fact, she found herself looking forward to it all through the day. Despite the shot of electricity when their hands accidentally touched, she felt more comfortable around him now that sex was no longer in the equation. In a few more months, she tried to assure herself, it would almost be like it had never happened—almost.

That is one thing she had decided while away from the ranch: this was home now, and this was her family. It was sad that it had taken her this long to find a family, but at least she finally had. She wished, not for the first time, that her mother had not kept her away as a child. She had been thinking about this recently, wondering what exactly about the West had kept her mother away for so long. She knew her father had been a "no good cowboy." Why this had to mean that all things west of the Mississippi were banned, she could not understand. Lenora knew that she herself had been born with an innate love of horses; she imagined that it must have come from her father. What had that man really done to her mother to make her leave and never come back? It was time that she had a good long talk with Annie about the whole situation. It had been long enough since her mother's death that she felt like she needed some answers.

Annie met Lenora inside the ranch house with a cup of hot peppermint tea and some fresh scones. Her aunt smiled shyly and led Lenora into the kitchen. All across the kitchen table were pictures. Many of them were black and white and some were splotched and sun faded. Shocked, Lenora touched her throat and could not speak. It was as if her aunt had been reading her mind and knew it was indeed time for Lenora to know more about her own heritage. Sitting down, Lenora felt the odd sensation of seeing her kin caught in snippets of time. She knew the images could never capture the whole of her lineage, but hoped they would at least give her a glimpse.

"This is your Uncle Byron's daddy, and this is his grandfather," Annie said.

She held up a snapshot of a tall boy wearing pants he had clearly outgrown. Standing behind him was a severe looking cowboy in his early twenties. There was nothing but dirt, a few stunted pines, and a very thin saddle horse in the background.

"This is Byron and his brother, Jake. Jake died in a car wreck in '72," Annie said.

Lenora slid the picture across the knotted pine of the kitchen table. Her uncle looked goofy and happy, his brother standing next to him was smiling with bigger ears than Byron and more freckles. Beside them stood another boy holding a fishing rod. He looked about the same age but with serious eyes.

"Who's the other boy?" Lenora said.

Her aunt in reply pushed more photos across the table. The dark eyed boy was riding a flashy palomino, holding up a big buckle that he must have won from a rodeo. Another photograph depicted him dancing with a girl at a county fair. Lenora thought she looked familiar.

"He's your uncle's cousin, Amos— a cowboy," Annie said.

Annie was looking at her hands and not at Lenora. "Your Mom and I argued over this often when you were young. And argued again when she was close to the end. She thought it was best you didn't know anything about him. He was a cowboy. You know, Lenora. The kind that chases girls, ride bucking horses and never earn more than they can drink on a Friday night."

"So he's my dad?" Lenora said.

"Yes," Annie said.

"Is he still alive?" Lenora asked. "Does he live in Montana?"

"Yes." Annie looked up, and Lenora could see anguish and worry in her aunt's eyes.

"Could I meet him?"

This was so much to take in. Lenora realized she had been gripping the solid oak of the chair back. She unclenched her hands and took a deep breath. It made, she realized, perfect sense to learn about her father now as she was building her own life in the mountains. She wondered for a moment if she did in fact want to meet this drinking, womanizing cowboy. She realized she did. Maybe he was different now, maybe he was not the man her mother loosely described with such distaste.

"You can," Annie said. "He'd like to meet you. I wanted to wait until you had had some time to adjust to everything before I brought him up. Are you mad?"

"No, no!" Lenora said. "I'm just kind of…. Well, I don't exactly know what to say. I didn't think that you knew who he was."

"Your mother was determined to have a better life," Annie said. "And I don't think she wanted anything holding the two of you back. She really was just trying to protect you and give you the best possible life. I'm sure of it."

"Mom always made it sound like she had a one-night stand or something," Lenora said. "I guess I just kind of hadn't even thought about trying to find him now that I'm older. I went through this period in eighth grade when I thought that he would come rescue me because Mom had this new boyfriend I hated."

Annie was crying and Lenora stood up and put her arms around her aunt.

"Annie, what's wrong?" Lenora said.

"I just wish that she hadn't been so stubborn about bringing you here. And I wish that I hadn't been so stubborn about coming to see the two of you in Chicago."

Lenora grabbed the box of tissues from the counter and made her aunt a fresh cup of tea. Annie wiped her face and then smiled at Lenora.

"You know I was mad at her at one point for never having another child?" Annie said. "I wanted one so bad.

And Byron and I both had problems. After the third miscarriage, well…. Well, Byron took matters into his own hands and went in and had 'the old snip, snip.' He did it so that I couldn't be hurt anymore by losing the babies."

Lenora was shocked by the deep sadness she witnessed in her aunt. More of the puzzle of her own ancestry was coming to light. Along the way, she was also beginning to see the complex dynamics between her mother and aunt.

"I was mad at your mother because she had you so easily and early, and I couldn't have a child even after waiting and being married and all that. You see, Lenora, Maura was the wild child, and I was the good older sister who waited to kiss boys and ride in their trucks. I played by all the rules, and yet somehow I was never able to have the children I so badly wanted."

"You have me," Lenora said. "I know I'm mostly grown up, but I still like it when you take care of me."

"You really are staying? Clay or no Clay?" Annie said.

"No cowboy is going to run me off." Lenora kissed her aunt lightly on the cheek. Annie showed Lenora more pictures of her mother wearing a daisy print dress and holding up a pet rabbit. Then older in a full bathing suit but with the body of a very pretty young woman. Towards the back of the stack was an image of Amos and her mother together. Maura looked like some kind of seventies movie star, with her bell bottoms and lovely full hair. Her father, Amos, had on tight jeans. His paisley shirt was undone to the fourth button, and he wore spurs and a cowboy hat. He had that look about him which Lenora was getting to know. It was the mark of a true working cowboy; serious with an easy air of confidence. He definitely was not just some dressed up dandy.

"What happened, Annie? What happened between them?" Lenora said. "What made Mom so mad?"

She touched the picture of her mother and father and felt a thrill run through her whole body. Never before had she thought she would actually see her father. Now to see both of her parents together, it was almost too much to believe.

"He was flirting with girls at rodeos when your mom was pregnant," Annie said. "He was a boy really, and I don't think he realized how much his life was about to change. They argued, and somehow it ended up that she moved away, and he never got to know you. Although, I know he came around one of the first summers she brought you back. That's part of the reason she stopped coming."

"So I met my dad?" Lenora said.

"Yes," Annie said. "You were only a year or two old though. It was so long ago."

Lenora did not really know how to feel. She kept picking up images and asking questions. Before she knew it the men were taking their boots off and coming in for dinner. Lenora jumped up from the table and started heating soup and cutting wedges of homemade bread. The men must be cold and hungry, she thought. Annie was telling Clay about some of the images, and she saw her uncle pick up a black and white photo. She wondered if Clay knew her father. Their eyes locked across the table covered in pictures. Lenora's hand stilled on the soup spoon, and her heart began to pick up speed. He nodded, his hair fell forward to cover part of his face and he looked back down. The moment passed and she could breathe again.

All through dinner Lenora felt like she was in a daze. Her mind tried to piece all the new information together. If only Maura had opened up to Lenora about the past. Why could she not have shared the truth about Lenora's father with her before she left this world so suddenly, Lenora wondered. Would even an irresponsible father have been better than leaving Lenora feeling like an orphan adrift in the whole, huge world?

The next morning dawned clear and bright with an inch of new snow covering the fields. Before doing chores or making breakfast, Lenora saddled Major. He was not happy about being ridden before being fed, but once he had a lung full or two of cold mountain air, he was fully on board with their illicit early morning adventure. She trotted him carefully up the drive to the west, which rose slowly to the summer grazing grounds. He was skittish in the cold, so she eased into a canter, burying her hands in his pure white mane and letting the chill air bring tears to her eyes. Far up the road, Major skittered to a halt. Two gray wolves crossed the road in front of them. Their muzzles were covered in frosty snow. Lenora imagined they had been digging in the fresh white stuff looking for mice or voles. Major watched them with his ears perked forward, and then he lowered his head and blew hard through his nose. Lenora could not help but laugh as both wolves silently disappeared into the pine forest to the south. She heard the crunch of snow behind them and Major swung around and whinnied as Clay came into view on a young chestnut. Lenora sat quietly on Major and watched him approach. The snow flew up from the long-legged colt's canter, and Clay's black hair blew back from his high cheekbones and dark eyes. Her heart bounced around her chest awkwardly. She tried her best to arrange her face in an appropriately calm and friendly expression for their sudden meeting. The only image in her mind was the firelight glowing on his tanned, golden-brown chest and the look in his eyes as he kissed every inch of her naked body.

"I'm sorry if I'm disturbing your ride," Clay said.

"No. It's fine," Lenora said. "We were just enjoying the snow and clear air. Oh, and two wolves."

"They come through this time of year," Clay said. "Usually from Canada. We don't have a pack near the ranch right now."

Lenora felt awkward for a moment but let Major fall into stride with the colt. The sudden, unbidden image of their lovemaking had left her with nothing to say to her handsome companion. She was relieved that Clay seemed inclined to let the silence of the morning settle around them.

The sun was full in front of them as they rounded another bend in the road. Snow shimmered in the pines and a few bare-limbed aspen. This was a perfect morning. They rode on in silence for another quarter mile, then Clay turned the colt, and they all headed back to the ranch. About halfway down the long road, she finally felt her head return to the moment and words were easier to find.

"Annie tells me you know my father?" Lenora tried to keep emotion out of her voice.

"I do," Clay replied.

She glanced over at him sitting his horse with such relaxed poise, and saw him carefully arrange his reins and smooth the copper hair of the colt's mane.

"He works at a small spread about forty miles from here," Clay continued. "Lives on the ranch in his own trailer. He works cattle and always has a decent saddle horse or two he rides."

She could hear in Clay's voice the masculine way of saying that this other man, her father, was a cowboy and not to judge him by outside standards. Cowboys were their own breed as she was slowly learning.

"I could drive you over later this afternoon? If you wanted to go?" Clay sounded hesitant and yet hopeful.

Lenora felt her insides freeze up as if she had broken through the iced over river and fallen into the cold, rushing water beneath. So soon, she found herself thinking. Should she really go at all, she wondered. Would he even want to see her? Did she really want to get to know this man, whom her mother had so studiously kept from her? She pondered this last thought. Clay did not break the silence. Once back at the ranch, he offered to take care of the horses so she could start on breakfast. Walking to the ranch house, her head was still whirling from the idea of seeing her father today.

Her aunt was outside helping with an early calf, so Lenora had the kitchen to herself. She scrambled some eggs and put slices of bacon in the oven; every once in a while, she surprised her uncle with bacon, and then poured the banana nut muffin batter she had mixed the night before into the baking tins. She definitely wanted to meet her dad. There was no doubt of that in her mind. However, she was scared to jump right in without first going over every possible scenario in her mind in agonizing detail. How would she even respond to him, she wondered. What should she call him: *Amos? Dad?* Would he be angry with her mother? Surely, he must know Maura was dead, and Lenora was here at the ranch, and yet he had not tried to come and visit her. Was he afraid after all these years? Or maybe Amos, like Lenora herself, was lost as to how a relationship could be forged between two adults who were tied together by such a strong bond, and yet complete strangers to one another.

During breakfast, talk of the sudden appearance of a new calf dominated the table. Lenora avoided Clay's eyes all through the meal, she really did not know if she could explain to him her fear of meeting her father without crying. The last thing she wanted him to see was how fragile her hard-won peacefulness really was.

After breakfast she and Jesse went out to the converted bunkhouse. The electrician had come and put in the new light fixtures and the elk antler chandelier. The area now was divided into two bedrooms and a large living room with a fireplace. The room had windows facing west toward the mountains and the sunset. Lenora set Jesse up with the cream paint, and she took the rich red and started on the accent wall opposite the windows. It felt good to stretch her back and watch the color glide on.

Later, as she opened bales of hay and fed out big flakes of delicious alfalfa, Clay came up beside her and opened the gate and then closed it behind her. They stood for a moment and watched the horses eat against the backdrop of the setting sun. Standing this close to him, with the length of the day behind them, Lenora wanted to lean against him and feel his arms slip around her. She imagined for a moment what it would be like to go back to his bunkhouse and let him just hold her, which was all she really wanted. He shifted next to her, and rested both arms on the cattle gate. She took a deep breath.

"Could you take me to meet my father?" Lenora said.

"On Saturday morning?"

He turned and looked at her. His eyes were so rich she imagined she was lying on her back looking up at a clear, night sky. It frightened her, and she looked down at the dirty snow under her boots.

"Yes," he said. "I would love to."

CHAPTER TWELVE

Awake with anxiety before the sun rose, Lenora baked muffins. She wrapped one for Clay to eat in a paper towel and then pulled on her coat. Outside, the icy chill of a gray day greeted her. Clay had the truck warmed up and waiting and she slid in and slammed the door on the dreary cold.

"For you, if you want?" Lenora handed him the muffin, still steaming from the oven and a thermos of coffee.

"Bribery?" Clay said.

"Or payment."

Her words sounded pinched to her own ears; she felt nervous and did not want to joke.

Clay ate the muffin by the time they had pulled out on the main road. Mechanically she offered him another from the basket.

"So good," he said between bites.

Lenora looked at her hands, which were sweating and white from being clenched together.

"Deep breaths," Clay said.

"I'm fine." She was instantly irritated he could tell how distraught she really was.

"I didn't say you weren't fine. I just meant relax. I imagine that he's way more nervous than you are. You hold all the cards, Lenora. You can, as you women always do, let him know where the relationship goes. I imagine he's just happy to know that you want to visit him."

He took his eyes off the winding road and glanced over at her as he spoke.

"Sorry," she said.

"No problem." His eyes were back on the road.

The mountains opened as they drove southeast, and the snow scape flattened and broadened. Lenora kept her eyes on the window, forcing her brain to register the changing terrain. She told herself over and over that she was the one in control; just like Clay had said.

Finally, they turned down a dirt drive and drove under a simple arch made of old telephone poles with the Double B's of the ranch name swinging in the damp wind. The road, like many ranch roads, led back a good mile and a half before they reached the calving sheds and a cluster of simple barns. Lenora noticed her shallow breathing and forced herself to take a deep lungful of air. Clay stopped the truck and shut off the engine, then put on his jacket and hat. He waited until she was standing beside him, before setting off for the biggest of the barns. Lenora felt eternally grateful that he was shepherding her through this introduction. The sliding door was open on the south end of the barn. They stepped inside to hear a radio playing Willie Nelson. A couple guys were standing around watching a man shoe a big gray mare. Clay shook hands with the lounging men. Lenora watched the man, shoeing the horse, straighten up and give her a very shy smile. He had dark eyes, a thick beard and skin that was tanned the color of weak coffee. He brushed his hands off on his shoeing apron and then took the few steps to Lenora.

"Amos," he said. He offered her his hand.

"Lenora," She said. Her hand was only a little damp as he folded it in his.

"You want to wait in the trailer?" Amos said. "I only have the right hind to finish."

Clay nodded and then guided Lenora out of the barn and

back into the gray day. They walked towards a grove of aspen, now naked and white trunked in the snow, and an ancient but solid trailer.

Inside, a very old cattle dog with foggy eyes and a limp greeted them amiably. The trailer itself was sparse but clean. The whole place smelled of saddle soap, which Lenora quite liked. She sat on a coach covered by a Navajo blanket with black and red and gray stripes and petted the dog. Clay banged around in the kitchen with a teapot and mugs.

"Tea or coffee?" He asked.

"Tea." The back of her throat felt dry.

There were a couple of Native American prints and a few pictures of horses and one of a group of cowboys all sitting on a fence and grinning. Lenora heard steps outside the trailer and then knocking of boots to remove snow. She felt her body tense up. The dog jumped off the couch and limped to the door, and Amos patted his head as he took his jacket off. Clay rose and handed him a cup of coffee from the counter and then offered him a muffin from Lenora's basket on a tiny paper plate. Amos took both and sat across from Lenora in a faded floral armchair. Unsure what to say she waited for him to speak.

"Well," Amos said. "I sure am glad you came."

He set the cup of coffee on the floor and brushed some crumbs off his lap, which the dog snuffled up. Amos looked right at her; she saw that his eyes were still the deep brown of the young man in the pictures.

"I don't blame your mother for what she did," Amos said. His voice was quiet and steady. He continued to pick each word with great care. "She only wanted the best kind of future for you. The best kind of life."

"I know she did," Lenora said. She felt the tears coming and was powerless to stop them. "You know she's gone. Right?"

"Yeah," he said. "Annie kept me up to date."

"I'm sorry, Amos," Lenora said. "I thought this out in my head a million times over. I thought I would tell you all about me and about my life. And now, and now I don't have a clue what to say."

The tears were coming. How had she turned into such a sodden mess, she wondered. Awkwardly, Amos stood and touched her shoulder. She was not sure how to respond, a hug seemed like too much too soon, and so she just reached up and touched his hand. His skin was warm and dry and felt comforting under her damp and shaky fingers.

"Sorry," Lenora said. "I'll be fine."

Amos sat back down. Clay slipped in next to her and lightly placed his arm around her shoulders. She realized Clay was treating her like one of his scared colts, she did not mind at all. No wonder all those horses loved him so much, she thought, he was a perfect security blanket.

"I was wondering if you would like to go for a trail ride next Sunday?" Amos said. "Clay tells me you have a nice Arabian, and you like to ride?"

"Yes," Lenora said. "I'd love to."

Riding would make this easier for both of them, she reasoned. Maybe she would not even cry.

"There's a little trail that goes up to this waterfall," Amos said. "And this time of year the elk are up there sheltering and feeding. I think you'd like it."

He was looking at his hands, and then slowly raised his eyes and met Lenora's tear smeared ones.

"I would," Lenora said. "Clay's been showing me this whole western way of riding and seeing the mountains."

She felt herself flush and hoped that her father had no idea about the romantic trail ride, which had led to their brief fling.

"The weather isn't going to get any better," Clay interjected. "We had better head on home."

They all rose, and Amos shook Clay's hand. Lenora impulsively grasped both of her father's hands in her own before turning and stepping out of the trailer into the misting cold. Amos followed them out.

"Thanks for the muffins. Very, very good," he said. "Clay,

thanks for bringing her."

"So next Sunday?" Lenora said.

"About ten or so in the morning," Amos replied. "I'll be waiting."

Clay and Lenora walked to the truck and climbed in. The air around them was turning to crystals and when Clay started the truck the windshield was covered in a thin layer of ice. Clay drove with deliberation as they left the ranch and pulled out on the highway.

"Will you help me move some horses around when we get home?" Clay said.

"Yes, of course," she said. "What's wrong?"

"I just don't like this weather. It's strange," he said. "Ice is the worst killer, snow is nothing compared to ice."

Feeling drained and relieved, Lenora sat back in the truck seat and was again thankful Clay had driven her.

"How do you feel?" Clay asked.

"Good. It's a relief really. Like I faced my fear. I don't know how I feel exactly about building a relationship with him. It's... Well, it's awkward and strange. But I like the idea of riding with him." She hesitated for a moment. "You will come, too, right?"

"Yes, I'll come," Clay said.

She thought she saw him smile, but he did not take his eyes from the sleet-covered road. She felt childlike as she suddenly realized she knew very little about Clay's family. It was ridiculous really, she thought, in the beginning she had been so shy around him and wrapped in her own veil of grief, then full-headed lust had taken over and there had not been room for much else.

She wondered if he would be offended if she asked now, so late into their relationship. The only time they had spoken of the past had been to share little tidbits from their childhood. Clay could be so quiet and private; making it hard for her to tell what was going through his mind. The funny thing about facing the fear of meeting her father was now Lenora found herself willing to take another risk and ask Clay about his own history.

"So, what about your dad?" Lenora said.

"What about him?" His voice was even.

"Where is he? Do you speak with him?"

"He was in South Dakota," Clay said. "Last time I talked to him."

"When was that?"

"Two winters ago."

"Clay, I'm just trying to know a little about you," Lenora opened her curled fingers and massaged the center of her left palm.

"I know, I know. Sorry. I'm really glad you and Amos met. He's a pretty decent guy." Clay glanced away from the road for a moment, his eyes were serious and dark.

"Thanks. It's still a little strange to *even* have a dad," she said. "So, you don't talk to your father much?"

She knew she was searching, maybe crossing lines that should not be crossed. Still she would keep digging a little further; maybe Clay would open up a tiny bit to her. He was silent as they crossed over the last big highway and ascended into the mountains. Finally, after she had given up hope and was about to try and find something on the radio, he began to speak.

"My dad is a real asshole. You know he has at least three kids spread across the west and no child support for any of them. But even more than the money, no relationship. The only reason him and I even talk is because there for a bit I was riding some nice cutting horses, one of them was this big-time stallion. Well, I got him a couple breeding's for next to nothing. And he had a pretty good colt, and I agreed to ride it and sell it as a futurity horse. Anyway, as soon as he got the money he left town and wouldn't return any of my calls. When we finally see each other, down in Scottsdale, he tries to dodge me. When I asked why, he admitted he thought I was after a cut from the colt. That just flat pissed me off. You know? Like my own father just thinks the only thing I want from him is money? Sure it would have been great to get a few bucks and put new tires on my truck. But what I really wanted was to know *my* dad. I wanted that pretty bad at points, growing up. All the other kids around me had dads with ranches and cattle and horses. And I didn't have anyone to teach me anything," Clay said.

Outside the sky was the same color as the road and Clay drove with both hands on the wheel.

"I can't imagine why he wouldn't want you in his life, Clay. You're what every cowboy should be; an honest man who tries to take care of everyone around him."

"That's kind of what your aunt and uncle keep on telling me," Clay said. "I've come to peace with who he is. I like to think I would have been a very different kind of father."

Lenora mulled over the image of Clay holding his child. He would be careful and gentle, she imagined, treating the baby properly, like a small gift from God.

"I'm sorry, Clay." She was at a loss for words.

"Me too. Every single day," he said. "But thanks." For one quick second he took his eyes from the slick road, she felt her chest constrict with the gentle sorrow she saw in his face.

"So, so, your mom...?" She said. There was a lot she wanted to ask him now that he was letting her in.

She remembered the long trip to check the summer pastures, and how she had opened up to him so much over those couple of days. Really, he had never returned the favor, and so she felt blindfolded while stumbling over his feelings and scars. If she was not going to make love to him, she at least wanted to know what was in his mind and heart.

"My mom is Lakota. My father a white man," Clay said.

His answer drew her out of her window-brooding, and her face was on fire. She did not have a way with words.

"I didn't mean their ethnicities!" Lenora blurted out. "I meant do you talk to her?"

"You white people are so worried about saying the wrong thing. Now that all the damage has been done." He flashed his full smile, and then continued. "Yes, I do. I will go and see her in the spring for the equinox ceremony. And before you ask, I last saw her when you took your trip back east. I have a brother, too, Corbin. He's out playing 'rodeo cowboy' right now."

"Oh. I see," Lenora said.

"I hope you get to meet her one day," he continued. "She would like you."

His words made her throat constrict. She could not help but wonder what he might have told his mother about her.

Glancing quickly at Clay, she realized he was now concentrating on the road which was too smooth looking. They fishtailed into the gravel driveway of the ranch. Lenora felt Clay visibly relax.

At the house Lenora pulled on her Carhartt's and a thick hat. Then she hurried out to help Clay move the livestock around. The ground was slick and the air full of ice.

Clay and Lenora walked up the wash to the west and opened the gates to let the horses into the North Barn. The group was a ragtag bunch of older ranch horses and some colts Clay was bringing up. The world around them finally gave way, and the temperature fell enough to turn the freezing rain to snow. Heavy, wet flakes fell all around them created a curtain into which buildings and animals disappeared. Lenora was shocked by the amount of snow falling so quickly.

Annie came out on the porch and made her way over to them. She brought a steaming thermos, and they all took swigs of spiked hot chocolate.

"So good! What is it?" Lenora asked.

"That's her secret recipe," Clay said.

Taking a large gulp Annie just laughed. Lenora felt giddy with the snow and alcohol; she could not help but love her first blizzard.

Much later, sitting around the fireplace with more mugs of Annie's magic drink and the snow falling outside, Lenora told them about meeting Amos. Her uncle whittled, and Clay worked on the fringe of his chaps with a large needle and thin strips of cowhide. Annie was quiet with a novel tucked between her legs, and Lenora felt herself give in to the peace of the evening. Their best herding dog, Suzie, slumped asleep at Lenora's feet. She reached down to run her fingers along the dog's silky ears from time to time during her retelling of the day's events.

"It was strange," Lenora said. "I had thought before meeting him that somehow I might recognize him. Like, well, like in a physically way. But I didn't. Well, maybe a little with my nose."

"And your eyes," Clay said. "But yours have flecks of green where his are just brown."

Lenora caught her aunt and uncle exchange a look. She felt herself blush, Clay still noticed her eyes.

Later in her bedroom Lenora watched the snow fall from the window. She smiled to herself remembering how well Clay had taken care of her during her first meeting with her father. At least she still had the beautiful cowboy in her life.

CHAPTER THIRTEEN

The horses breathed steam as the sun rose and filtered through the pines to the east. It was Sunday, the day of the trail ride with her father. Clay held the door to the horse trailer and Lenora untied their two horses and backed them out. Before they had time to wrap legs and throw saddle pads over the horses' backs, Amos had pulled into the gravel lot in a blue and rust Chevy with a small, gray horse trailer behind.

Lenora realized this was her father. The thought made her heart tighten. Having gone through so much life without this parent, it seemed like a strange gift to now have him.

She watched as Amos climbed out of the truck and took off his hat as he approached. Her mind began racing as she wondered if she should hug him or shake his hand. She had no idea.

Thankfully, he stopped on the other side of the horses and nodded to Clay and then looked at Lenora. She could see as much worry and unease in his eyes as she was sure reflected in her own— this was not easy for him either.

"Hi, thanks for asking me to come riding today," Lenora spoke first.

"Of course," Amos said. "Sure am glad the weather decided to hold. It's a pretty ride up, but not much fun with sleet in your face."

Clay had moved off and adjusted the rigging on his saddle. Lenora suspected he was giving her space and tried to be thankful, not terrified. Who knew that relatives, especially long-lost parents, were the scariest social encounter, she thought.

"This your Arabian horse?" Amos asked.

"Yes," she said. "This is Major Temptation."

Amos picked up her horse's hooves, looked in his mouth and ran his hand down all four legs. Lenora knew he was trying to connect with her in the only shared thing they had at the moment— a love of horses.

"Well, he's no quarter horse," Amos said. "But those are some good strong legs and hard hooves."

Lenora smiled, that was the closest she was probably ever going to get to a compliment for her horse from a true cowboy like her father.

"Let's see your horse," Lenora said.

"I bred and raised him myself." He rested his hand on gelding's withers. The horse sniffed at Amos's sleeve.

Lenora could hear the pride in his voice and wondered again why her mother had never shared this man with her.

The three of them rode single-file up the winding, mountain trail. Hemlock branches hung in thick curtains making their trip up seem like an enchanted journey. There were moments where the sun shafted through in pure brilliance. Lenora ran her hand through Major's mane, letting her fingers catch on a snarl.

Nearly forty-five minutes later they reached the top and let the horses stand and blow. Lenora sucked in her breath as she saw the sun glance over the frozen falls. Wave upon wave of perfect, clear glass gave way to rings of milky ice. The waterfall was suspended in winter splendor. She climbed down from her horse and walked to the rocky ledge. The sight of the easterly sun caught in thousands and thousands of crystals took her breath away. She felt a man approaching and turned to find Amos standing beside her. She could not help but look back, searching for Clay. Their eyes met. She wondered how she would ever repay him for being her silent and strong friend. For a quick moment, she wished they could be standing here alone, as lovers again.

The thought faded, and she realized she had been given the greatest gift: she was getting to know her father.

"It's breathtaking," she said.

Amos smiled and turned to her, his eyes no longer seemed so unsure. They could find common ground. It was not too late for a relationship to form, grow strong.

Late Monday night, tossing in her rumpled bed sheets, Lenora realized what she had to do in the morning. She had already planned a trip into Missoula for the following day. The timing was right.

Before anyone was awake, she fed the horses and laid out two loaves of banana bread on the kitchen counter. It was still dark as she turned on the truck headlights and headed out of the ranch. A jackrabbit darted across the hard-packed snow just before she made it to the paved road, its ears flat back against it small skull. Driving with her knees, she undid the lid of her big thermos and smelled the richness of coffee, vanilla and coconut oil— her favorite morning beverage, with an extra-large portion today, since her night had been far from restful. The sun rose as she listened to a mix of the morning news and Hank Williams Jr and Willie Nelson. Her first stop was the huge furniture store on the east side of town. She found the linen curtains she wanted and also two heavy end tables. The mattresses she had ordered the month before had arrived, and she drove the truck around to the back of the store to load them up.

"You have someone at home to help you unload these?" The bigger loading guy asked.

"Yes. I sure do," Lenora answered. How wonderful, she thought, that she had a whole assortment of family back at the ranch. After being raised an only child with one parent, she was finding family a true luxury. Of course, knowing Clay would be at the ranch helped as well.

Finally, her last stop— the fancy grocery store for the few things she could not source closer to the ranch. It was now close to eleven A.M. and time to make the call. She pulled the crumpled piece of paper out of her pocket and dialed the number. Her mouth was suddenly so dry that she could not swallow, but she did not hang up. She remembered the isolation and fear she had experienced stranded along the mountain highway with a flat tire. She had breathed her way through a tire change and out of the emotional wreckage of her previous life— she could do this. The phone range four times. She almost thought it would go to voicemail, and she could forget her whole stupid idea.

"Hello" on the other end.

"Um, Crystal?" Lenora said.

"Yes. Who is this?"

"This is Lenora, from, from Bear Dance Ranch? My aunt and uncle and well, well, Clay lives there?"

She felt lost, rambling. What was she thinking, she wondered, ex-wives were not flat tires.

"Oh, yeah. I know who you are," Crystal said. "Why are you calling me?"

"I was actually wondering if we could meet," Lenora said." I know it's weird. I just need to talk to you."

"Yeah, sure. You want to come to my place?" Crystal said. "I'll text you the address."

Then the line was dead, and her phone beeped at her a moment later with the street numbers. Lenora was shaking. She closed her eyes and took three deep breaths, which sort of worked to calm her nerves. She closed her eyes again and pictured Major's sweet face and then galloping him through the valley next to the ranch. That was better, she could drive. She started the truck and drove east along the river, then through campus and to a run-down apartment complex.

Lenora looked through her grocery bag and found a bottle of espresso and coconut water, maybe this would be a good gift. Feeling ridiculous with the coffee, and yet convinced she needed to bring something, Lenora knocked on the door. Crystal opened immediately and waved Lenora inside. The living room was filled with two potted plants and a huge blanket made of native designs hung on the wall. Lenora handed Crystal the coffee and coconut water mixture and watched the puzzlement on Crystals face give way to a smile.

"I really like this brand," Crystal said.

"Yeah, me, too," Lenora said.

"Want to sit down?"

Lenora sat on an under-stuffed couch, covered with another blanket close in color to the one on the wall. Crystal went into the kitchen and returned with two glasses of water.

"It's all I have," Crystal said. "Unless you want whiskey?"

"No, this is perfect," Lenora said.

"So," Crystal said. "You're here to ask me about Clay?"

Lenora took two gulps of water. Crystal was watching her. The woman was more beautiful than Lenora remembered ,her dark hair a curtain falling around her bare, sleek shoulders.

The pang of pure jealousy that shot through Lenora's belly surprised her. This woman had made a baby with Clay.

"So, you want Clay?" Crystal said. "That's why you're here. To ask me what's between us?"

"Yes," Lenora said. "And, also, to ask you to come to dinner at the ranch. If you want."

Lenora was grateful for the other woman's ability to speak the truth, even though she detected an angry edge to the words. How must she look to Crystal, she wondered? She was the new woman entering late into the story of their lives and losses.

"He's picked you already," Crystal said. "About time he should pick someone. We ended a long time ago." She swooshed her long hair back in a fierce gesture. "I left him a long time ago. I don't like those ranches so far out. I don't like the mountains bearing down. I don't like being away

129

from other people and then coming into town and blinking like moles just surfaced. I don't like his life."

Lenora felt it too as she came into the city that morning, her brain amazed by the traffic and speed of everyone hurrying. She had recognized it even more when she returned to Chicago. Maybe, she thought, this was why her mother had fled the mountains and the solitude. Though, unlike Maura and Crystal, Lenora felt herself melting into the wildness and loving the new shape her mind and emotions took as they formed to her life at the ranch.

"I think my Mom must have felt the same way. Though she never spoke of it to me," Lenora said.

"Oh, yeah Annie's dead sister," Crystal said.

Only then realizing her harsh words, Crystal looked Lenora straight in the eye.

"I'm sorry. I'm sure it's hard to lose your mom and all," Crystal said. "I lost mine when I was pretty young, so I don't really remember her. But still it's hard."

"It's actually embarrassing how hard it was for me," Lenora said. "I felt really weak and silly for a long time. I was this depressed slob who cried all the time and lived on frozen pizza."

"Yeah, I know the feeling," Crystal said. "Clay's been like, the only real family I've had in a while. That's why I still go and see him. You know? When I'm lonely."

"I don't know if he told you?" Lenora said. "But I overreacted when you came to stay last time. My ex-husband was unfaithful. And I, well, I felt threatened. I'm late to know all the details and history out here."

Crystal picked up a pack of cigarettes lying on the table next to the jade plant and flicked out a single white stick. Her fingers were long and delicate. Lenora watched and mulled over Crystal's last words.

Lenora was just starting to realize how rough Crystal's childhood must have been, no wonder she was drawn to Clay; most flight creatures like horses were. Clay had a way of making the world seem small and bite-sized , Lenora thought, no need to tackle all of it in one day. Just a few short months ago, she had been in Crystal's position: no family, no husband and the whole world in front of her.

"Maybe," Lenora said. "You would like to come and have dinner on Christmas Eve? I was going to cook something special, and Annie is making pie. It might be nice."

She had no idea why her face was getting hot, she could only imagine what she must look like with her red appearance and her freckles all mapped out across her cheekbones.

"None of my business," Crystal said. "But I think you still have a thing for him. Why else would you show up at my place? I don't imagine you're here to make friends."

Lenora was silent for a long moment. She looked down at her clasped hands in her lap and gathered her thoughts as best she could. "Like I said before; my ex-husband was not faithful. I guess I don't trust very easily now. Plus I've only been divorced for a year."

It was actually almost two years, Lenora thought. In many ways the marriage had been over for a year or more *before* that.

"I'd really like you to come for Christmas Eve dinner," Lenora said.

"Yeah," Crystal said. "I might. I do like coming out every once in a while. I don't work at the diner anymore. I'm at the casino near Polson now. Better money, you know? So I guess I'd be closer. Wouldn't be much of a drive over after work."

"Okay," Lenora said. "So it's settled. Christmas Eve. Around six o'clock or so."

Setting her empty water glass on the card table Lenora stood. Crystal stayed seated. Lenora's heart was racing, but she made it out of the apartment door and down the single flight of stairs and to her truck. She wondered if everyone could see that she was not over Clay Darkhorse. Perhaps she should have accepted Crystal's offer of whiskey.

***

Three days after Lenora's meeting with Crystal, the first guests arrived at Bear Dance Ranch. Lenora pulled off her apron and hurriedly washed the last of the flour off her hands. Out on the front porch she met the Reynolds, with their two teenage sons and a large Labrador Retriever.

Lenora's stomach was in knots but she took a deep gulp of the cold air and smiled. "Welcome to Bear Dance Ranch," she said.

"This is so beautiful!" Both the husband and wife exclaimed at once.

"Jake Reynolds. And my wife Jennifer. Our boys Todd and Kevin," the husband said.

"This is so much prettier than your pictures online," Jennifer said. "Once we pulled off the main road and started towards the ranch, we had to keep pinching ourselves that the place was real! The snow is so lovely too!"

Lenora no longer had to try and smile. This was going to work, she realized. She turned to find her Uncle Byron and Aunt Annie standing on the porch behind her. She saw them suddenly through the eyes of the newcomers: Byron with his heavy, oiled coat, wooly chaps, cowboy hat and wild rag. Annie had her hair in a braid and beautiful silk scarf and long wool coat. She wondered where Clay had gotten to; he would fulfil the guests' dreams of the Montana Cowboy.

Amazed, she watched her aunt and uncle become cordial hosts. Before Lenora knew it the whole group was in the kitchen eating muffins by the hearth. Then the Reynolds drove their car down to the converted bunkhouse. Clay appeared around the side of the barn on a stocky bay gelding. The light snow had caught in Clay's shoulder length, black hair, and his eyes stood out dark and strong against the pale blue sky. Lenora's heart jumped in her chest; Clay looked like a painting sitting on his horse. Lenora heard Jennifer's surprised, "Who is *that*," from behind her.

Clay dismounted and shook hands all around. Of course they loved him, even the teenagers put away their phones to touch the gelding's nose and smile awkwardly at Clay. After everyone had petted the horse and been promised lessons tomorrow morning in the arena, Lenora led the way into the refurbished bunkhouse. The hardwood floors had been sanded down and refinished; they were the color of an old whiskey barrel. Heavy carpets in natural colors highlighted each room, and the furniture was old but carefully restored. The linen curtains were thrown open to highlight the true centerpiece of the living room, floor-to-ceiling windows. They revealed a stunning view of the river twisting around the foothills of the west pasture and the glittering snow covered mountains.

Lenora turned to see the expressions on their faces; she had done well. The looks of admiration and delight were perfect affirmation.

"I'll leave you to get settled in. Dinner is at seven, and I will bring it down," Lenora said.

Back in the ranch house she worked on a salad with arugula, toasted pecans and chunks of roasted butternut squash. She drizzled maple syrup vinaigrette over all of it. Polenta with goat cheese and shitake mushrooms, steamed asparagus and small but perfect cuts of steak filled up the large, white plates.

Lenora covered all the food and set the trays on the heated mats before putting on her parka and making the trek down to the bunkhouse. She was efficient and polite and left her guests with plenty of food and instructions to leave the dishes in the hallway. In the ranch kitchen once again, she dished up the remaining food for dinner. The high from the arrival of her new guests was wearing down, and she was tired enough to wish she could skip dinner and just take a hot bath. Tomorrow would be an early day, with barn chores to be done and then breakfast for nine hungry people. But, oh, was it worth it. The three-day stay of her guests would bring in as much as three heifer yearlings sold at auction. This was the beginning of better times for Bear Dance Ranch, she just knew it.

CHAPTER FOURTEEN

Christmas Eve dawned clear and bright, the light snowfall from the night before left the whole ranch dusted in a sparkling blanket. Lenora was worn out but happy as she made the final breakfast for her departing guests. After arranging the trays with the French press, maple-pecan scones and hot apple preserves, as well as frittata of goat cheese and chives, she made her way through the snow to the bunkhouses. Her days had started at 5 am since her visitors arrived. The early mornings just meant she was alone with the horses and the beautiful mountains before anyone else was awake. If this was her way of saving the ranch from the doom of being parceled off and sold to build mansions, then she would get up even earlier and never complain.

As soon as she knocked on the bunkhouse door, Jennifer Reynolds opened it and welcomed her into the spacious foyer.

"We've all had such a marvelous time here at Bear Dance Ranch. I really hope that you will have us back someday soon," Jennifer said.

"Oh, yes. Please do come back," Lenora said. "And if you wouldn't mind telling your friends about us as well, we would really appreciate it."

Jennifer turned and gave her husband a quick look.

"Well, actually," Jennifer said. "I'm a travel writer for *Vente Magazine,* and I wanted to do a story on your ranch. The timing seemed right, so I brought the whole family with me for a pre-Christmas trip. I really, really loved the ranch, and your family and the amazing food. You should be a chef in New York City. Do you know how well you could do with all this clean-eating, organic stuff?"

"Thank you!" Lenora replied. "The article will help us so much, and I'm so glad you enjoyed my cooking. I used to doubt my ability, but coming out to this ranch has saved me, as well as my passion for cooking. And so you see, even if I went to New York it wouldn't be the same. I owe everything to this ranch and the people on it, and so I'll stay here and cook."

"It's so refreshing to meet someone as dedicated to what they love as you are," Jennifer said.

Back inside the ranch kitchen, Lenora poured herself a cup of coffee and added a dash of vanilla and coconut oil. Annie appeared around the doorway with Clay and Byron behind her.

"Looks like our guests had a great time," Annie said.

"Yeah, they really did," Byron replied grinning.

He came over and kissed Lenora on top of her head before picking up a scone and giving her a wink. Lenora was so happy and surprised; she put her hand on top of her head to feel where her uncle had kissed her.

"Oh, man. We have a dude ranch," Clay said.

"Whatever it takes," Annie said. "Now eat and then out. Because Lenora and I have a whole Christmas dinner to put together."

By one o'clock in the afternoon Annie and Lenora had a pineapple-glazed ham in the oven. They also had prepared a sweet potato casserole and a vat of cauliflower mashed potatoes. They also had roasted brussel sprouts with an avocado oil glaze, three pies and two dozen dinner rolls.

Byron entered the kitchen with a big smile and Jesse at his

UNDER THE MOUNTAIN STARS

heels. Both looked hungry and a little frosty from the wind.

"How about I head to town," Byron said. "And pick up your friend Liz?"

Lenora realized Liz's plane would be landing in just two hours. How had the day gotten so busy?

"That would be amazing," Lenora said. "There's still a lot to do for dinner."

"We'll head out now," Byron said. "Clay's stripped the sheets in the bunkhouse. And I think he's even vacuuming. Just help with the tractor when he takes hay out to the heifers, please."

"Of course I will," Lenora said. She smiled, thinking of Clay doing laundry.

At ten minutes till five o'clock, Lenora abandoned the kitchen. Everything was finished or nearly so. In her room, she sat for just a moment to enjoy the peace of the setting sun out her bedroom window. She was exhausted but so happy. This Christmas was proving to be so much cheerier than the previous one. For a brief moment she went back to that gray day a year earlier. She saw herself sitting on the couch in her mother's empty house, hitting reject on the calls from her worried friends. The day had slipped past as if on some kind of horrible slow loop.

She realized that was in the past, but she felt like if she did not look back from time to time she might take all of the new joy and people in her life for granted. Never again did she want to take for granted how precious every second with those she cared about truly was.

As Lenora came down the stairs, she saw that Amos had already arrived. He had taken off his hat, and he smiled as soon as he saw her making her way down the staircase. Lenora wore a soft, cream dress with a green angora sweater over the top. Before she could lose her nerve, she gave Amos a quick hug. He looked surprised and pleased. Just then the door opened, and Liz came through with her glowing skin and huge smile. She was followed by Rosa and her husband

Landon, then finally Clay, Byron and Jesse.

Hugging and kissing ensued; it seemed that Rosa and Liz were already hitting it off royally. Annie ushered everyone into the living room, and bottles of red wine and Byron's favorite bourbon were opened. The doorbell rang again and this time Jesse's parents, the closest neighbors to the south of Bear Dance Ranch, were at the door with more wine and a very thick pecan pie.

"I can't believe how beautiful it is out here," Liz said, once they finally had a moment alone in the kitchen.

"I know," Lenora said. "I still wake up sometimes and have to pinch myself."

"You look awesome," Liz said. "I really, really mean that. You look like you're actually happy again."

"That's funny you would say so, because when I was upstairs getting ready I was remembering how bad last Christmas was. Just how sad and lost I felt. I'm really, really grateful that I made my way out here. Oh, and get this; the lady who brought her family out to stay at the ranch this last week, is a writer for *Vente*. Can you believe it? We're getting a write up! Bear Dance Ranch is getting a write up in *Vente!*"

"Wow!" Liz said. "That's awesome."

"I know, I can't believe it. I just really want to make this whole guest ranch thing work. I want to do my part, you know?"

"Yeah, for sure," Liz said. "So, I hate to change the subject, but is that *the* Clay that you told me about?" She nodded towards Clay, who was laughing and telling some horse story to Amos, Byron and Jesse's father.

"Yeah, that's him," Lenora said.

"Wow," Liz said. "He's a hunk. You kept talking about how he rode horses well and all that stuff. But you never said that he was so sexy!"

Liz was starring; Lenora could not blame her. Clay looked amazing; he wore a black, fleece shirt with a blue button up underneath. His hair was free of a hat and brushed the collar of his shirt. It was impossible, even in the two shirts he wore, to avoid seeing the strength in his broad shoulders, the tapered waist that led down to his rider's butt and long, lean legs. Just then, Rosa appeared.

"Who are you two ogling?" Rosa said. "Oh, right. Clay. He's easy on the eyes for sure."

"So is your husband, Rosa," Liz said. "I think I need to move out here. Since getting off the plane, every man I meet looks like he just walked out of the pages of *GQ: Western Edition*, like he could kill a bear and build a fire with a piece of flint!"

As if realizing he was the object of their discussion, Clay turned and came into the kitchen. He held a tumbler with a fingers' worth of amber liquid. His eyes were alive with the fire and dancing shadows in the room.

"Hi Ladies," Clay said.

He was the gentleman and took Liz's hand and smiled his full, white grin at her. Lenora was pleased to see that even man-savvy Liz looked a bit like a deer caught in the headlights as he held her hand.

Just then the doorbell rang again, and Lenora had a feeling it was Crystal. It was. Annie shepherded Clay's ex-wife into kitchen.

"Lenora invited me," Crystal said quickly, almost defensively, as she pulled off her coat.

Clay turned to Lenora with his eyes full of questions. Lenora smiled and took Crystal's coat and scarf.

"I'll explain later," she said quietly to Clay as she passed him.

Liz followed Lenora to hang up the coat.

"Let me guess, that's the ex-wife?" Liz said. "You invited her?"

"Yeah. Look at her," Lenora said. "Why does she have to be so gorgeous? And need so much from him?"

"Dinner!" Annie called.

Lenora tried to quiet her thoughts and began pulling dishes out of the oven. She really hoped Clay would be pleased she had invited Crystal. Their hands met as she handed him the glazed ham. She felt the familiar jolt and held his eyes for a brief moment.

Once everyone had filled their plates, they returned to the large table. Byron had added both of the leaves to enlarge it enough to fit all their guests.

"Thanks everyone," Byron said. "For coming to Bear Dance Ranch tonight to help us all celebrate Christmas. I really want to thank my wife, Anne, and my niece, Lenora, for making all of this amazing food. You both have outdone yourselves. You're spoiling us rotten. Merry Christmas!"

Lenora blushed and looked down at her plate. When she looked up, Clay was watching. He winked, and gave her one of those lopsided smiles that she loved so much.

The food was good, the wine wonderful and having Liz and Rosa at the ranch made the evening perfect. On top of that, to have Christmas dinner with her own father... how life was changing. Lenora knew she was smiling uncontrollably, but she could not help it. Amos sat on her left and his voice was intimate and warm as they spoke.

"How was it having your first guests at the ranch?" Amos said.

"Actually, really good," Lenora said. "They loved the place and said they would come back. Mrs. Reynolds writes for a travel blog and so I think we will get some good publicity from the stay. Clay was pretty patient as a trail guide, even though I know it's not his life's aspiration."

"That's great news," Amos said. "I'm proud of you for having a strong vision for this ranch. How's that horse of yours getting along?"

How wonderful it was to have a father who asked about her horse, she thought. Smiling, she took a bite of brussel sprouts; they were tender and had a slight tang from the fresh rosemary and avocado oil she had used to roast them.

"Thanks for having me over. You're one hell of a cook. And it's pretty nice being with family for Christmas," Amos said. He looked down at his plate and shuffled his fork from hand to hand as he spoke.

A lump formed in her throat; part joy at the budding relationship with her father, and part sorrow to realize that, as she moved forward, the memory of her mother changed and shimmered differently in her mind. The future was full of surprises and somehow that made the past a little more bearable, she thought, even as it shifted.

By the time pie was served with coffee, everyone had moved to the arm chairs around the fire. Clay and Byron had brought out their guitars and Jesse's father had a harmonica. Soon, lively country classics filled the ranch house. As the evening wound down, they played "Silent Night," and Lenora and Annie sang along.

After catching herself yawning for the second time, Lenora left the group to put the pies away. Clay followed her into the kitchen.

"I can get it. Enjoy yourself," She urged, trying to take the dirty dishes from his hands.

"Don't be silly, I can help," Clay said.

They put food away in the refrigerator and stacked dishes in the sink. Sounds of "Jingles Bells," and uproars of laughter came from the other room.

"Thank you for inviting Crystal," Clay said.

"Sure, no problem. You know I went to visit her a little while back?"

"Really? No, I didn't know that," Clay said. "Why?"

"Well," Lenora said. "I guess to get to know her better. I know I overreacted that first night she showed up here at the ranch. I'm still sorry about that. I'm starting to realize that my whole reaction had everything to do with me and my past. And, well, really not much at all to do with you and Crystal."

He stopped rinsing dishes and turned to look at her, his face more earnest than she had seen him before. She set down the casserole dish and met his eyes, even though her own were a little blurred by tears.

"I guess I should have told you that I still took care of her," Clay said. "I would have never slept with her after our camping trip." He looked down at the soapy water. "I would have reacted just like you did if it had been your ex that showed up. I'm so sorry."

"It's just that at the time I was still so raw from my divorce," Lenora said. "From my mom."

She waved her hands in the air and felt the tears really prick her eyelids. Blinking quickly, she leaned against the sink to look out at the clear night. Stars and half-moon lit the fields of pure white.

"I'm sorry. I really, really want you to trust me again," Clay said. "I wish I could go back and change a few of my actions. I wish I could have seen how this would affect us."

He reached out and touched her shoulder. His hand felt warm and alive with all the electricity Lenora remembered. She turned from the window into his arms; it was like coming home after a long trip. He sighed as she laid her head against his chest. He brushed his hand up her neck, under her hair. His finger sent shocks of pleasure through her whole body. She looked up at him knowing she toyed with fire. He had been waiting, as soon as their eyes locked he bent and kissed her. She responded by kissing him back; that was all the permission he needed. He deepened the kiss, devouring her lips. His tongue was strong and fast as it stroked through her mouth. She could not breathe and grasped his arms, enjoying the movement of his biceps under her hands. His hands reached down and cupped her buttocks before lifting her up so that she was straddling his waist. With her in his arms, he turned and perched her on the sink. Her skirt hiked up, and his emboldened lips kissed down her neck. He pulled her sweater free from her shoulders and exposed her bare skin, then lipped his way along her arms and collarbone. Lenora was lost in his touch, unabashed as she threw her head back and enjoyed the play of his tongue across her body.

"Um, wow, sorry."

Reality came back with a rush. Lenora pulled her sweater back up her arms, her face on fire. Clay let her slip to the ground and turned shielding her from a laughing Rosa and Liz.

"Get a room, you two," Rosa said. "Or at least go upstairs."

"Sorry, it was the wine," Lenora said.

"Really?" Clay said. "Just the wine."

"Yes. Um, no," Lenora replied. "I don't know."

She was flustered, confused and a little angry to have been caught by her friends. She had let her guard down. It was easy to keep everything friendly between herself and Clay until they spoke so openly. All her buried feelings had risen quickly to the surface with his frank words.

She straightened her dress and walked past Clay, trying to resist meeting his eyes. He touched her arm, and she turned. His eyes were full of questions.

"The party isn't over yet," Lenora said. "Let's have another drink."

Out in the living room, the party definitely was still swinging along. Annie was dancing with Amos and both were pretty light on their feet. Liz and Lenora sat down on the long couch. Landon grabbed Rosa as soon as they entered the room and pulled her into the dance. Clay was somewhere behind them, and Lenora watched as Crystal found him and pulled him into the fray. There was no reason to feel jealous. After all, she was the one who had invited Crystal, she reminded herself.

When Jesse and Byron started playing the next song, Clay grabbed both Lenora and Liz and pulled them up and into the spinning mix of bodies. Out of breath and red-cheeked, her jealousy forgotten, Lenora began to smile.

After the dance she noticed Crystal head off to the bathroom. She knocked on the door after a few minutes had passed.

"Are you okay?" Lenora said.

"Yeah, just a long day and too much wine," Crystal said.

"Would you like to go lay down for a while?" Lenora said.

"Yes. That would be perfect," Crystal said.

The two of them made their way upstairs. Lenora helped steady the taller woman as they reached the landing.

"I drank too much again," Crystal said. "I always do that at the wrong time."

"Yeah me, too," Lenora said. Pulling back the two quilts and flannel sheet, she readied the bed for Crystal.

"That first time you came out to the ranch, do you remember? Well, I went into town and sang karaoke with Rosa. And made a huge fool of myself by drinking *way* too much. Clay came to collect me, and I was foul-mouthed to him."

"He's used to it. I got so drunk a few times, he had to carry me to the truck," Crystal said. She pulled off her jeans and climbed into bed.

"I'll get you some water," Lenora said.

Outside in the hallway she was amazed at how easy it was to be nice to Crystal when Clay was not around. Actually, she realized, she even liked the other woman. There was something child-like about her even while she tried to act so worldly. Could she really blame Clay for still feeling responsible for Crystal when she herself was now taking care of her after a few too many drinks? Funny, she wanted a man with a big heart in her life, and, yet, she also did not want him to be kind to his ex-wife.

Lenora set a full glass of water on the nightstand. Crystal had closed her eyes, but she opened them as Lenora was about to leave the room.

"Thanks for inviting me. I had a good time," Crystal said. "I won't get in your way. I promise. Plus, I don't think he loves me anymore."

"Okay then. Sleep well," Lenora said. She found herself smiling as she closed the bedroom door. She knew Crystal meant no harm with her tipsy words.

After their last guests had finally gone home; Rosa driving

her bourbon-sodden husband, Jesse, and both of his parents, Lenora and Liz sat down by the fireplace. Liz winked and poured Lenora another glass of wine.

"Sorry for walking in on you two earlier. I thought you and Clay were finished with all that," Liz said quietly.

"I was. I mean, we are," Lenora said. "I don't know what happened. We were talking and then he kissed me."

"It looked like more than just a kiss," Liz said. "And, it also looked to me like you kissed him back."

"I did. He's amazing," Lenora said. She took a sip of wine, thankful the day was over, and she had a friend to confide in.

"I don't think you see the way he looks at you, Lenora. He's still crazy about you. Why not give it another shot?"

"I don't want to ruin what we have. You don't know how hard we have had to work on getting our friendship back. It's been a long road. I just can't stand the thought of losing him, and that seems like the only likely outcome to me."

"Or maybe you married the wrong guy," Liz said. "When you were too young and inexperienced to know better. And, well, now when you have met the right guy, you're too afraid to commit again. Learn from your mistakes and move onward. Life isn't about a single shot at happiness. It's about trying again and again until we get it right."

"I think that's the most profound thing you've ever said to me." Lenora smiled at her friend.

"I just care about you," Liz said. "And I think Clay cares too. I know I'm just arriving on the scene and don't know all the past history, but I think you're a great person who deserves to be happy. You need a wonderful guy like Clay in your life!"

"Oh, Liz, I've missed you," Lenora said. "I'm not going to live in fear of failure because of Mick my whole life. I know I'll get brave again. I'm sure of it."

CHAPTER FIFTEEN

Christmas Day brought a pink infused sunrise. Lenora struggled out of bed and sat next to the window to see the sun light the mountains and snow-covered fields. As she looked down, she saw a small package wrapped with a white bow sitting on the window sill. Curious, she opened the package and found a silver pendant in the shape of a horse head. The workmanship was extraordinary, and when she turned it over "forever" was etched on the back. She hoped it was from Clay. She opened the clasp and put it on, letting the pendant drop under her shirt to lay hidden next to her skin.

Before Liz had to leave for the airport, Lenora and Annie saddled three horses and took their guest out to see the beautiful morning. The light made the snow glitter and the horses were eager, prancing and tossing their heads with joy to be alive on such a beautiful day.

"Thanks so much for having me at Bear Dance Ranch," Liz said. "This has been the best Christmas a city girl like me could ask for."

"Come again in the spring," Annie said.

Lenora smiled, wishing her friend could stay longer.

Late Christmas evening after taking Liz to the airport and caring for the ranch animals Byron, Annie, Clay and Lenora sat around the fireplace. Lenora was exhausted. The guests, her early morning and the huge Christmas feast had all been so much.

"Good news everyone, two days before our next guests arrive," Lenora said.

"So soon?" Clay said. "I feel like the Reynolds just left."

"I know," Lenora said. "But this is a busy time of year with the holidays. Look on the bright side; if we can do well this winter we can repair all of the fences along the drive and maybe renovate the shed into a kitchen and dining area."

"I'm getting used to the idea," Byron said.

"Me, too," Annie said. "Just so long as we have breaks to recover in between."

They all sat in silence, listening to the fire until Suzie got up and stretched her back legs. The dog wanted to go out. Lenora opened the door and let her out onto the porch. When she turned Clay was standing behind her. Heart pounding, she closed the door and looked up to meet his eyes. This was the first time they had been alone since their encounter in the kitchen the night before. Impulsively, she touched the necklace hidden under her shirt.

"Do you like it?" He asked.

"Yes." She wanted to say more but not sure she trusted herself.

"Would you come out to my quarters so that we can talk? We need a little privacy," Clay said. He nodded back towards her aunt and uncle in the living room.

"Now?" Lenora said.

"Yes." Clay's eyes were dark and hard to read in the dim light of the hall, but his face had the intense and determined look she was starting to recognize.

Lenora reached for her heavy coat and scarf. "I'm going out for a bit. Goodnight," she called to her aunt and uncle.

A few snowflakes drifted down to the white earth. Their breath was thick as morning fog as they made the short walk to Clay's quarters in silence. Inside the small but warm room, Lenora took off her outer layers while Clay added another log to the woodstove. Lenora sat next to the window. She pulled the curtain back to watch the snow fall and waited for Clay to speak.

"What was last night to you?" Clay's voice was so low that she had to turn towards him in order to hear his words.

"A mistake," Lenora said. She had to be firm in her resolve tonight.

"A mistake?" Clay said. "Really?"

He poked at the fire with a steel-tipped rod. She could tell he was angry.

"Clay," she said. "I'm sorry. I don't want to mess up what's between us."

"Oh, yeah? What is that exactly?" His voice was no longer low and soothing.

"I mean, I don't want to lose you as a friend and as the Ranch Foreman. I could never live with myself if my aunt and uncle lost you, because I couldn't keep my hands off of you!"

"I'm sorry, I guess I keep thinking if I give you time you'll change your mind," Clay said. "But you really think I'd be immature enough to leave Bear Dance if we didn't work out?"

"No, I don't. I just know how strange everything gets after a breakup. I mean, I don't want to worry about the future. Annie and Byron have been great by taking me in, and I don't want to mess everything up."

"Then don't. Just trust for once that life will work out. Ok? Come over here, and sit with me." Clay was not asking. "You act like you were some crazy stranger your aunt and uncle took in. You're their family. They love you. And you have more than pulled your weight around this place. You have as much value here at the ranch as I do, and you have to know that's the truth."

Lenora sat on the loveseat next to him and he put his arm around her. Her body did tingle at his touch, but she felt too tired to do anything more than lean her face against his chest. He put his other arm around her until she was enfolded in his warm, minty scent. Soon, her whole existence was his body holding hers, the firelight flickering on the walls of the tiny cabin and the beating of his heart under her hands.

She must have drifted off, because she woke as he lifted her and carried her to his bed. Such a shame, she thought that she had fallen asleep and missed a chance to simply be held by him. Now, even more than before, she cherished every second that he touched her.

"I can walk," she mumbled.

"I know," Clay said. "But you're tired. Plus, I like the way you feel in my arms."

She did not fight him as he helped her pull out of her jeans and sweaters. She smiled to herself thinking how he only ever seemed to see her in plain, cotton underwear. Then he stripped down. She could not help but watch the way his skin glowed in the warm light from the woodstove. He pulled on a t-shirt to sleep in and crawled in next to her. Lying still in his arms, she wished he would kiss her, touch her. But he lay still and was a gentleman and held her only as a friend. She turned her head away from him on the pillow and tried to only let a couple of tears soak into the soft flannel. She tried to remind herself this was what she wanted.

During the night she woke and rolled over. Her body was alive with the knowledge she lay nearly naked next to Clay. She slid her hand under his shirt and let her fingers explore his smooth skin. Nestling her face into his side, she breathed in his smell and was rewarded by mint, honey, saddle soap and the other musky smell, which was all him.

"Careful, Darling. Don't wake me up with those sexy hands of yours and expect me to lie quietly," Clay said. "Don't push your luck. I never claimed to be a saint."

"I thought you were asleep," Lenora said abashed.

She giggled a little and pulled her hands out from under his shirt. Actually she wished he would act first, initiate the intimate caress she secretly wanted. She could hardly be the first one to act, now that she had been so adamant they be friends and not lovers.

"So, when I'm asleep, you think you can do as you please?" Clay said. "How would you like to wake up and find my hands all over you?"

She knew she would love it, but saying so would not further her case. He rolled toward her, and they were suddenly face to face; though she could not really see his lips, she felt his warm breath on her cheeks and eyelids.

"I'm sorry for pushing you. But just know whatever you end up deciding about me and about us; I don't love Crystal anymore. I haven't for a long, long time. Though, I'll admit I've gone back to her a few times in the past. But, as I think you know, she's had a rough go of it. And in a lot of ways I'm the only real family she has."

"I realized that, finally. And so, I went to her apartment and invited her to the party," Lenora said. "I actually think we could be friends at some point in the future. I was pretty jealous of her in the beginning though."

"Why was that?" Clay said.

"Well, because of you. And because she's so pretty," Lenora said.

"You're very, very beautiful, Nora. I swear you don't see yourself in the mirror," Clay said. "Plus, you have one hell of a heart."

He kissed her gently on her forehead. She smiled, burrowing into him and the warm blankets.

"Thanks," Lenora said. "I think you have a pretty great heart too."

"I really hope you'll consider having me in your future," Clay said. "You just think about it and get back with me, okay? Just promise you won't use Crystal as an excuse anymore? We both know that you've been afraid to commit to me, to us. And that's only in part because of my ex-wife."

"Okay," Lenora said. "I promise."

Promising was one thing, actually coming to terms with

her fear about the future was another altogether. Funny, she thought, that Clay would see through her attempts to use Crystal as a diversion from her own fear of a new relationship. But of course he would, she thought, he read horses and cattle every day.

"Have you known for long that I'm afraid?" Lenora said.

He was quiet in the close darkness. She shifted against his body and felt the skin on the back of her legs tingle with joy at his nearness.

"I don't think I knew until you came back from Chicago," Clay said. "Picking you up and seeing the look of pure terror in your eyes made me realize what was really going through your head. I only wish you would have looked into my eyes. Then you would have realized I shared the very same look."

"Fear isn't something you just know how to control. Not just like that. Or at least I don't," Lenora said. She bit her lip and pulled away from him. He was acting like she had rationally decided to expect the worse outcome in their relationship; that was hardly how it had happened.

"I'm not saying you planned it, so stop getting so huffy," Clay said. He grabbed her as she pulled further away from him in the bed. "Come on, we're just talking. I'm just saying that I wish you would have told me exactly how scared you were. Maybe I could have assured you a little? Or at least, I could have told you my fears. We could have gotten it all out in the open."

"Yeah, well," Lenora said. "I was just trying to survive at that point. It's not easy getting a divorce and losing one's mother all within a year. And then, on top of that, I moved to a strange place and met a new guy who just so happens to still touch his ex-wife on the front porch after dinner."

She was angry and decided there was no reason to hide that fact. Pulling away from his arms, she sat up in bed her hair a wild mane of chestnut and gold. She arched her eyebrows and looked at his face in the half-dark to see what he would say in response.

"Touching my ex-wife?" Clay asked. "What? You mean

putting my hands on her shoulders? Touching means something way different, Darling. I think you know very well what my sort of touching does to a woman."

"You arrogant asshole!" Lenora was out of the bed and searching for her pants in the dark room.

"Wait, I'm sorry," Clay said. "I was just trying to be funny. Please don't go. I'll be deadly serious from now on. I promise."

He found her hand, then quickly drew her fingers up to his mouth and kissed her knuckles. She tried to pull away, still angry, but he jumped out of bed and stood behind her.

"You don't have to make fun of me," Lenora said. "I saw you touch Crystal in a familiar way. Seeing that sent all kinds of alarm bells through my head. I don't want to be with a guy who wants other women. I'd rather live alone for the rest of my damn life than be with a guy who will betray me and abuse my heart."

"Yes," Clay said. "I'm sorry if I ever led you to believe that I was untrustworthy. You can trust me. I'm kind of crazy about you, if you haven't noticed already."

The sound of the wind outside their cozy nest warred with the thundering of Lenora's heart. She took two gulps of air and decided she would have to forgive him. He was too earnest, she thought, and after so many months of observing him it did seem like he was telling the truth. Crazy about her, she thought, that sounded amazing. His fingers brushed against her cheek and tangled in her messy hair. The tingle of his touch had suddenly grown to a surge of pure desire leaving her toes and fingers trembling. Maybe he stepped towards her, or she towards him, Lenora had no idea, suddenly his arm was around her, and his other hand lifted her up. She responded by wrapping her legs around his body. He looked down just as she looked up; his lips were liquid, as fiery and pure as mountain moonshine. She opened her mouth to welcome his tongue and let him possess her soul. He was rough as he pulled off her thin undershirt. He tossed Lenora onto his bed and stripped away his own clothing.

Pulling her panties off, he threw them across the room. He nestled between her legs and kissed her as ravenously as before. Her whole body grew damp and hot as she wrapped herself around him.

The outside world slipped away as he turned her cold and tense body into a fine-tuned instrument, which only woke to his touch. She threw her head back and gasped for air as he moved away from her neck and down to nip and lick at her erect nipples. He suckled and teased and finally bit so that she cried out. Her body loved the mix of pain and pleasure. She felt the core of her heat pulsing between her wet legs. He ran his hand across her vulva and then slid his finger into her wet folds. She gasped and gripped his shoulder with her free hand.

"Do you like that?" He said. His voice was deep and raspy and full of the night and unabashed lust.

"Yes," she said.

His response was immediate and intensely gratifying, as two fingers breached the limits of her body, and then his thumb rubbed along her swollen clit. She gasped and felt his lips hot and rich on her throat and then her mouth. She kissed him back as if she could drink in the night and ward off tomorrow. She felt the velvet skin of his penis and she pushed him off of her with all her strength. Then naked with her hair a flowing mane of fire around her shoulders, she straddled him. Loving the feel of his muscles hidden just beneath his golden skin, she ran her hands over him, then turned and took the full breadth of his erection into her mouth. She felt his fingers brush along her backside, and hoped he was enjoying the view as much as what she was doing with her tongue. A gasping moan came from his throat, and then his hands pulled her back until he could lick her exposed clit while she suckled him. He pulled away first, effortlessly flipping her around so that he was above her, and they faced each other.

"Dear God, that felt so good," he said. "But I've been too long without you to play this game."

"You're mine tonight," she said. Smiling, she flicked her tongue across her lips. Tonight was outside of time and boundaries.

With her pulse hammering in her ears, and his naked body stretched beneath her, Lenora moved to take him in. He arched his back and thrust, and she was wet with hunger as she welcomed him and his man-*ness*. The night seemed to be one for dropped guards and full hunger. She reared back, his erection still buried deep inside of her. The change in position sent shocks of deep pleasure vibrating through her body, and her throaty gasp of desire brought an impish grin to his face. Then he moved; the rhythm deep and lasting with a steadiness of drums around the fire from times both past and present. Never before had any man made love to her as Clay did, now. She was his in a deep way that had nothing to do with traditions or society, and everything to do with passion so lasting the very mountains must be built upon it. Was this, she wondered, how the ocean and the land felt as they came together along smooth, sand beaches and rocky, irregular coastlines? She knew this coupling was more than sex and deeper than touch.

"Yes, yes!" She was shouting and damp with sweat, he thrust so deep she swore there would be nothing left of her. Yet still she pushed down onto him, and as the bolts of electricity shot through her delicate nerve endings; she came with the force of a tsunami.

They wrapped their arms around each other and held on, as if each were the last piece of driftwood in the shipwreck that was life. Slowly, as their breathing stilled, they held each other, the sweat drying on their tired bodies. Finally, sleep caught them, pulled them under together.

CHAPTER SIXTEEN

Bright sunshine woke Lenora. She rolled over in bed and realized she was alone. Her whole body ached deliciously. She wanted nothing more than to lie in his arms and luxuriate in the night they had just shared. Where was he, she wondered. A cold lump was forming in her stomach, she pushed it away. She got up and searched for her clothes and found a note on his nightstand.

Nora,
I'm so sorry to leave you, but one of my old training horses is collicing, so I have to take her to the vet hospital. Stay in bed, I'll be back!
C

How she wished she could stay in bed, but the day was fully underway. More than anything she wanted to talk with Clay a little more. She needed to hear from him again how he felt about her, before they dove back into their headlong love affair. Well, it might be a little late for that, she thought, as she examined a bite mark on her neck. Thankfully, she could wear a turtleneck this time of year.

Standing in the kitchen putting together a breakfast of

fresh strawberries and steel cut oatmeal, Lenora realized she had not called her father to thank him for coming to the Christmas party. Just then the phone rang, she picked it up to hear Amos's voice on the other end.

"Hi, Nora. I've got a mare that's going to foal tonight, and I wondered if you'd like to come and watch?" Amos said.

"Yes," Lenora answered. "That sounds amazing, what time should I come over?"

"Maybe around nine o'clock tonight," Amos paused. "It's hard to say when that mare will decide it's the right time. But I suspect it won't be before it gets good and dark."

"I'll be there," Lenora said. "Oh no! I have to go. I'm about to burn breakfast."

All day Lenora had been restless, hoping Clay would drive back from the vet hospital. Of course, she thought, he had left his cell phone sitting on the kitchen counter next to the coffee pot. She waited as long as she could before taking the truck over to do foal watch with Amos. She was careful to look for elk along the east bend of the river. Clay had told her the bulls liked to bring their herds down to water after dark. Playing with the radio dial, she finally gave up and hooked up her phone to the truck stereo and found her old playlists waiting like forgotten friends. Jack Johnson seemed perfect for tonight.

Lights were on in the horse barn when she pulled off the main road. The truck bounced through the snow-rutted drive to the ranch. Before getting out, Lenora pulled on her heavy coat, a silk wild rag and hat. Sitting around in a cold barn all night would definitely give her a chill if she did not dress properly. Amos met her at the barn door. His quick smile went straight to his hazel eyes. Even though she had hugged him at Christmas, they were not quite familiar enough to touch on everyday occasions. Low-light lit the foaling stall. A very pregnant mare stood eating hay. The horse lifted her head to give Lenora a steady look and then went back to the alfalfa.

"Stella is a pretty darn good broodmare," Amos said. "Back in the day, she was really something on the rodeo circuit."

"Has she had a foal before?" Lenora said.

"Oh, yes. A few," Amos said. "She's a good producing mare and easy to work around. A colt of hers sold a few years ago for more than a new dually truck."

"I've never seen a foal be born before," Lenora confided.

"Well, it's more waiting around than anything else," Amos said. "Mares can pick the time of the birth. It's a survival mechanism so that in the wild they can deliver their babies when it's safe and not when some hungry mountain lion is stalking them. So, that means Momma here will have this foal when she wants and not a moment before."

Lenora sat in a camping chair and Amos in another. He oiled old bridles, and Lenora tried to read the book she had brought. After a few minutes of reading the same page over and over, she put the book down and worked on menus. What she really needed to do was talk to Clay. Yet the next group of guests were coming to the ranch soon, and she needed to make shopping lists. Last night had been so amazing, she wanted nothing more than to be back in bed with Clay, warm and safe in his arms.

Close to midnight the mare left her hay munching to wander around the stall and lay down. Excited that the delivery might commence, Lenora stood.

"Better not," Amos said. "We don't want her to think we are interested."

"Okay," Lenora sat down and tried to get back into the book again.

The mare stood back up and began eating hay. Lenora sighed. This was worse than she had expected, and she was tired from her long day.

"How's Clay doing?" Amos said.

"He's fine," Lenora said. "Why do you ask?"

"I just thought things might be changing," Amos said. "For the two of you."

"Well they aren't," Lenora said. "I really wish people would stop assuming that we are going to end up together. A lot of couples don't work out. I know that. You should know that too. You and mom didn't work out!"

Amos was quiet, and Lenora realized that her tone had been too sharp, and her words were out of line.

"I'm sorry. I didn't mean to sound so rude," Lenora said. "I guess I've been on edge a little about Clay lately. I just don't know what to think." If only he had not had to leave that morning before she woke.

"I know you must think I'm out of place to ask about your life, after all these years. It wasn't my choice just so you know, I wanted Maura to stay. She probably made the right choice taking you away. I know that now. I wasn't much of a man back then." He rested the headstall of a bridle on his knee and looked up to meet Lenora's eyes.

"What happened?" Lenora asked. "I've wanted to know for a long time. But I didn't know how to ask."

"Your mom had dreams. Big dreams. And the grit to see them through. I was young and thought she should give up her dreams to let me pursue mine. Well, she thought that was pretty stupid and told me to my face. I let her leave with you, like the idiot cowboy I was back then, I thought she'd come crawling back when she ran out of money. She never did though, and my pride got in the way for a long time and so I never went to find the two of you," Amos looked at his hands. "Not my greatest moment, letting my woman and baby drive off for the big city all on their own."

There was a long silence as Lenora took in the missing pieces from her past.

"I did try and come find you," Amos continued. "Eventually. Just so you know. I wasn't a complete coward. But it was too late by then. Your mom had made up her mind about me and didn't want some ragtag cowboy holding her back."

"Wow," Lenora said. "I guess I had no idea that you even knew about me. She made it sound like I was the product of too much whisky and fun. Mom was always vague about the whole situation, like it was just the two of us, and that was all we needed. So, you saw me when I was a baby?"

"I sure did. You had the most beautiful smile, like the whole world was just pure magic, and you loved all of it," Amos said. He reached in the breast pocket of his coat and pulled out his wallet and then handed Lenora a faded photograph.

She saw her mother in bell bottoms and cowboy boots. Her hair a big frizz of curls around her face. Amos had a ridiculously long mustache and held a baby with its fist in the air. She had no idea there even existed an image of her with both her parents. How strange to be looking back on a time that she had no memory of, she thought, and yet she had imagined over and over for most of her life. Her eyes filled with tears. She had no idea if they were for her mother, whom she missed every day, or her father who she was just starting to realize loved her. Maybe, she thought, they were for her; she felt equal parts lost and found by this picture of the past.

The rustle of straw as the mare laid down brought Lenora back to the present. Quickly, she wiped at her eyes with the sleeve of her barn coat.

"She's having that foal," Amos whispered.

Quietly, they both stood and made their way to the stall. The mare with sweat-dampened chest, rolled onto her side just as a delicate leg, still housed in the gray, amniotic sack, appeared under her tail. The mare trashed around in the straw and took deep breaths. Then both of her hind legs stiffened as another contraction shuddered through her body. A head appeared and then another leg, with one final push, the foal's shoulders were through the birth canal. The rest of the body slipped onto the straw-covered floor of the stall.

"Go in quietly and pet the Momma on the shoulder," Amos said. "And then pull that sack away from the baby's nose."

Lenora hesitated for a moment, afraid to enter the stall and disrupt the beautiful moment. But Amos was insistent. "Go on now. Go steady."

The mare raised her head as Lenora entered the stall. Lenora carefully let the horse sniff her hands, before kneeling next to the bundle of legs and pulling the slippery amniotic sack from the delicate nostrils of the foal. As she laid both of her hands on the tiny ribcage, she felt a deep breath shudder thought the tiny body. The foal lifted her head and the legs kicked with life. The foal was perfectly alive and a filly.

After the little filly had wobbled her way to standing she nuzzled around her mother's udder to find the first gulps of thick colostrum. Lenora and Amos headed back to his trailer for a few hours of sleep before dawn. He had carefully made up his bed with clean, plain white sheets for her and a makeshift cot for himself in the living room. She was touched by his attempts to be a good father, even though she was far from childhood. Maybe, just maybe, she thought, it was not too late to have a father.

Bright sunlight was streaming in the window when she rolled over. It took her a moment to realize that she was in her father's trailer. She remembered back to the birthing of the foal the night before and the revelation of her parents' relationship mishaps. Feeling stiff and still very tired, she hunted for her phone on the floor in the pocket of her jeans, it was already 10 a.m. There were two missed calls from Clay, but when she tried him back his phone went straight to voicemail. Not unusual, she reminded herself, in the mountains, with so many no-service areas.

Outside the trailer a brisk wind lifted the loose curls from her forehead, and the smell of mud, churned up by the pen of heifers, filled her nose. Amos was inside the barn cleaning the birthing stall. He smiled when he saw her enter the dim barn. As her eyes adjusted to the low light of the barn, she saw the foal had filled out during the night. Her small body was already becoming round as the rich milk from her dam fleshed out her sides.

"She's a real beauty," Amos said. "Don't you think?"

"Yes," Lenora replied. "She is. I love the perfect blaze on her little face."

They were silent watching the mare gently nuzzle her foal as the little filly began to nurse.

"Thanks for letting me come over and be a part of this," Lenora said. "And thanks for telling me about you and Mom. I never knew any of that. I wish she would have opened up to me more about the past. That's one thing I guess I'm still mad at her about, for holding so much of the past from me."

"I bet she only did it to keep you safe," Amos said. "She was like a momma bear with you even when you were just a tiny thing. She wanted nothing but the best for you, and I'm sure she knew how hard a life ranching is and wanted something better. Don't blame her, Lenora."

"I know. I'm not trying to complain. I just sometimes wish that I could have known the whole story. What if I could have come out here for the summers? Stayed with you and Byron and Annie?"

"I don't know. She had her reasons, I'm sure," Amos said.

Before she could change her mind, Lenora leaned in and hugged her father, pitchfork and all.

Halfway back to Bear Dance Ranch, she stopped at a little gas station. The rust-bitten sign for diesel fuel was swinging in the kicked-up wind. As Lenora pushed through the glass door, a little bell rang, and the cashier turned towards the light. Lenora thought for a moment the small woman with braids was Susan from the airport. How strange the mind acted with lack of sleep, she thought. The stand with fresh brewed coffee was right next to the cash register; Lenora poured herself a big cup and then paid.

"Long night?" The dark-eyed cashier said.

"Yes," Lenora said. "A foal was born. A little filly."

"What color?" The lady said.

"Chestnut with a white blaze," Lenora replied.

"That's a good omen to be sure," The lady said. "The fire mare. I bet she'll bring new beginnings to everyone who touches her life."

Lenora pressed back out into the sunshine. Her last year had been filled with new beginnings. What more could change? Clay. Instantly, her mind was filled with the smell of him as they lay in the cave after making love. She stopped with her hand on the door of the truck. To lay with him again, she thought, to not fear the future and just love him, that would be a welcome change. Crystal was a thing of the past. All that stood in the way of the two of them trying to forge a future together was Lenora's own worries and fears.

She pulled the truck door open and headed home.

Suzie met her as she climbed out of the truck, whining and wanting her ears scratched. Lenora pulled her coat and gloves on and then turned to see Jesse running towards her from the barn.

"They took him to the hospital," Jesse gasped. "Annie said you should come."

"What?" Lenora said. "Took who? Who did they take?"

"Clay. That two year old colt flipped over on him, and he got all banged up. It was a hell of a wreck, Lenora. Really, really bad," Jesse said. He was white-faced, his brows pinched in the middle.

No, please don't let this be happening. But it was happening. She climbed back in the truck and roared down the dirt road. The day had gone from beautiful sunshine to sharp daylight; the kind that does not leave any life unexamined. The miles were slow to slip by, even as she pushed the truck to new speeds on the winding roads. Finally, she forced herself to drop the speedometer needle below fifty-five mph and take a couple of deep breaths. From a logical standpoint, she knew there was nothing she could do to help Clay. This was not her area of expertise; she was helpless when faced with a broken body.

Close to the lake, she gained cell phone service and

fumbled with her phone.

"Lenora?" Annie said.

"How is he?" She tried to make her voice sound calm.

"We don't know. Byron is trying to get some news from the duty nurses, but we really don't know anything."

"I'm coming. I just passed the first turn off to the lake so I'll be there soon," Lenora said.

"Please be careful. I know you haven't slept much, and I don't want you driving fast."

"I'm going slow now. I promise."

Her mind was clear and her body rigid with fear. Maybe before her mother's diagnosis, she would have believed that nothing bad could ever really touch her. After the disease, death and lonely pain, Lenora knew all too well that she was not safe; no one was. Clay was human, and, like her mother, could leave the world with speed and little fanfare. Lenora had lost faith in the invisible safety net she once believed kept those she loved safe.

By the time she locked the truck doors in the hospital parking lot, her hands were shaking so badly she could hardly hit the button on the key fob. *Please let him be okay, please let him be okay,* she repeated over and over in her mind. Multiple times during the rushed drive, she had tried to picture Clay smiling, sitting astride Moon, his teeth flashing white and hair tousled by the wind. Each time she had the image just right it would split and splinter, and she would instead see him broken on the ground, his face pale as late winter snow and eyes closed to the world.

At the entrance to the hulking, sandstone building Lenora had to force herself to stop and read the sign. She hated hospitals. The last thing she wanted was to be lost. At the Emergency Room Desk, the nurse took an eternity to check the computer screen before sending Lenora up to the Surgery Floor. Once again, she waited as another nurse stared at another monitor before being escorted back to a small waiting room. The walls were decorated with outdated prints of cowboys and skinny looking horses. There were no windows.

Annie jumped up from a tan chair and rushed over to wrap both her arms around Lenora. Byron engulfed both women in his big arms. He kissed Lenora on top of her head, as was becoming his custom. Within the warm embrace of safety, Lenora felt her throat close and the first tears fill her eyes.

As everyone separated Annie said: "He's in surgery. We don't know anything except a concussion, collapsed lung and a lot of internal bleeding. There may be more we just don't know yet."

"What happened?" Lenora said.

"That Pritcher Lady brought over a colt that had been acting up. Clay worked with it for a while and then got on." Annie said. "The horse reared and went over backwards. Landed right on him."

"Oh, Clay," Lenora whispered.

Byron was silent and deep lines were etched on either side of his mouth. Annie looked older, too, Lenora thought, she felt her heart start up an irregular fast beat.

After more coffee than was advisable and a lot of sitting and pacing and sitting again, all three were close to giving up hope.

"Maybe it's good it's taking so long?" Annie said.

"I'm sure you're right." Lenora fidgeted with a piece of torn skin on her finger.

Byron was silent. He sat with his hands on his knees and his gray, felt hat hooked over his thumbs. He met Lenora's eyes. There was something scared and young looking in his expression even though his face had aged during the long, horrible day. Lenora knew Clay was the son Byron had never fathered.

How silly her fear of betrayal seemed, she realized, as she stared potential loss in the face. Somehow, she always thought she and Clay would end up back together. Mistakenly, she had imagined they had all the time in the world to reconcile. Time was fluid, and like the river next to Bear Dance Ranch, it sometimes ran slow and languid and other times ran over its banks with urgency.

She knew she had been a fool not to tell Clay she loved him.

The surgeon appeared in blue scrubs with a mask dangling around his neck. He looked tired in the harsh light, and his glasses had a smear mark on them.

"Mr. and Mrs. Ranvier? I'm Doctor Clark. Clay is resting, he's not awake yet, but he will be soon. He had a pretty long surgery, but I'm hopeful that we've fixed him up pretty well. He should be just as good as new, with a lot of rest and physical therapy."

Lenora felt her whole body implode with relief. She felt so dizzy that she quickly sat down, skittering the plastic chair across the linoleum and making a horrible screeching noise. Her aunt rested her hand on Lenora's shoulder as she tried to listen again.

"...Punctured lungs, which can lead to fluid buildup. The right ulnar was fractured in two places, but the titanium plate will secure the bone," Dr. Clark said. "You can all make your way over to recovery, and you can see him very soon."

Lenora felt warm relief filter slowly through her body. It felt like hot tea after a cold afternoon outside in the wind and snow. Now, she thought, if only she could quiet the frightened voice in her head, the one that was reliving the terrible afternoon as her mother slipped from this world.

A brisk lady with a tablet computer in her hand appeared and led the three of them to the recovery rooms. She pulled back one blue sheeted area and there lay Clay, his face was pale and black hair damp on his forehead. Lenora stood frozen as her aunt and uncle gently touched his hands and face. He was dressed in a blue hospital gown with white strips. Her eyes traveled over him, trying to access the damage to the rest of his body.

She had the overwhelming urge to curl up with him on the upright bed, just wrap her arms around his broken body and make the past six months disappear. In reality though, she stood just outside the curtain and watched as he slowly opened his eyes. Her aunt started to cry as she brushed Clay's black hair back from his face. Byron was smiling and holding Clay's undamaged hand, and they all looked so happy and relieved. Lenora could not believe her own fear was still so heavy in her chest. He was looking around her aunt and uncle; he found her eyes with his own. Clay's half smile was slow but steady, and her heart nearly broke with her own foolishness. Why, she wondered, had she not let herself fully love this man?

CHAPTER SEVENTEEN

"Did the mare have her colt?" Clay asked

Now it was Lenora's turn to feel her throat close and the tears come, they were so scalding hot she could not blink fast enough to keep them from spilling down her cheeks. She stepped into the tiny room. His eyes never left hers, steadily drawing her towards him.

Still she could not speak, and so she took the hand Byron released and Clay offered. He squeezed her fingers in return and still met her gaze. She had to look down and swallow before speaking. "Yes, she had a chestnut filly."

"It's good luck having a filly," Clay said. "And red mares always bring change."

"Clay, I'm so sorry. I..." Lenora did not know what to say.

"I'm going to be fine," Clay said. "A few bones to heal. And the lungs already feel much better. You should have seen Byron's face on the way to the hospital. He drove that dually truck like a formula-one car."

"You should have seen your face, Clay," Byron said. He reached out and touched Clay's shoulder and then looked down to hide his own tears.

A nurse appeared and ushered them out of the curtains,

and then a tall lady with Clay's clear, bright eyes came walking down the hallway towards them. A taller, younger version of Clay flanked her. Lenora knew she was staring, but the young man must have broken a lot of hearts with his clean jawline, dark complexion and shining, black hair free-falling down his back.

"Raina," Annie said and grasped the woman's turquoise studded hands.

"And you are Lenora?" Raina said. "Clay's told me a lot about you."

"Yes, I'm sorry we're meeting under such bad circumstances," Lenora said. Her voice sounded stiff even to her own ears, and she felt her cheeks starting to heat up under the older woman's steady gaze. Now she knew where Clay got that piercing look, his mother.

Raina smiled and then turned and pulled open the curtains, despite the nurse's protest. She knelt next to her son's bed and kissed his damp forehead and touched his cheeks and neck. Lenora could not hear what she said to him but felt the warmth only a mother can give to her own dear child.

When Raina appeared again and stood with their small group, her eyes were softer. "I'll stay with him tonight. You all should get some rest," she said. "Ahh, sorry. Lenora, this is my youngest son, Corbin."

Clay's brother took Lenora's outstretched hand and held it while meeting her eyes. "My brother spoke the truth when he said he had met a woman as beautiful on the inside as the out."

Lenora just stared at him, unsure what to say. He released her hand, and then he moved to his brother's side.

"Let's go home," Annie said. "We all need to sleep, and we can come back first thing in the morning."

Despite the slow pulse of a headache, Lenora did not want to leave Clay. What she really wanted was to sit with him quietly, to show him she loved him more than she feared a broken heart.

She needed a quiet night to say those words to him; a night to ride in the mountains, to feel the brush of stars and the smell of pine sap on the breeze. Instead, she went to his bedside, and with the nurse, his mother, her aunt, uncle and his brother all watching she bent and kissed his pale lips. When she pulled back his eyes were open, and that half smile she so loved slowly appeared on his face.

"Maybe I should tell those young colts to try and kill me more often." Clay said. "Seems you like me better hobbled and in bed."

Was it her imagination, she wondered, or was he flirting with her in front of his mother. Her face was hot, and she could not look up from the bedsheet.

"Please, don't ever let it happen again," Lenora said. "What can I bring you for breakfast?"

"Blueberry muffins," Clay said.

The next morning everything conspired to keep her from the hospital. She woke to hear Uncle Byron yelling that the heifers were loose. Outside in the pre-dawn light, a herd of twenty young mothers stood around the ranch house leaving piles of steaming manure in the snow. The ranch had guests arriving that morning; Lenora sighed and zipped up her coat. Next, Jesse complained of a stomach ache, and two minutes later he was outside leaning over the porch and releasing breakfast. The morning kept getting worse: Raina called the ranch and informed Annie she was taking Clay back home with her to recover.

Lenora felt like crying. All she wanted was to spend the afternoon sitting with Clay at the hospital, finding out that he might not be returning to the ranch for weeks, maybe longer, was too much to handle. The whole situation was a huge mess. Lenora slammed down the colander in the sink.

"What's wrong?" Annie said.

"Nothing, sorry. I think I'm just out of sorts from not getting enough sleep and being all stressed out about Clay."

"Byron and I are going to see him in just a little bit, want to come?" Annie said.

"Yes, I, I just have so much to get done," Lenora said. What she really wanted to say was she needed to be alone with Clay.

"Go," Annie said. "We managed the ranch before you showed up, and I bet we can even manage these guests as well. Now go!"

As Lenora entered the hospital room, she was met by Raina and Crystal. Corbin stood at the window, looking out at the parking lot and mountains in the distance. Lenora felt her stomach clench into a cold ball of dread. She wanted nothing more than to shut the door, slip back down the white-squared linoleum floors and out into the bright sunshine. Instead, she closed the door behind her and leaned against it. She met Clay's beautiful, deep brown eyes; her stomach unclenched enough to do a quick flip. It was good to see him, she thought, even if he still looked tired and beaten.

"Hi everyone," Lenora said. "I just wanted to stop by, and make sure Clay was getting along okay."

"Hi," Clay said. He patted the white, hospital bedspread beside him as an invitation for her to come and sit with him.

"It's good to see you, Lenora," Crystal said. "Tell Annie and Byron hi for me. I better get going, my shift at the casino starts really soon."

"Bye," Lenora said. She realized she was even more jealous and protective of Clay now that he was injured.

Lenora sat next to Clay on his thin, hard bed. She pulled out carefully wrapped blueberry muffins from her purse and laid them on the table.

"You brought them," Clay said. "Thanks."

"Would you like a muffin, Raina? Corbin?" Lenora said. "The hospital food really stinks."

"Yes, it does. Those look amazing," Raina said. She reached out her hand for a muffin and even smiled a little. "I can't wait to get him back home with me, and then he can heal up proper."

Lenora met Clay's eyes; she knew her own eyes must have been huge with worry. Her mind was filled with doubt.

"Just for a month," Clay said. "That way you don't have to take care of me and everything else around the ranch."

Lenora looked at her hands. The one thing she did want to do was take care of Clay.

"Clay tells me you have a dude ranch now out at Bear Dance?" Raina said.

Was it Lenora's imagination, or did everything this woman say seem like a challenge. Had she been like this to Crystal, or was it because Lenora was a white woman? She felt ridiculous for even thinking that way, but Raina was pretty darn chilly towards her.

"Yes, we do" Lenora said. "The ranch needed another source of income. The cattle business doesn't always bring in enough money to keep the place afloat."

"Clay also says that you don't even eat beef?" Raina said.

"No, I don't," Lenora said. She felt caged and locked her fingers together, Clay touched her knee, but she did not look at him.

"The beef business has been bad for the west. My people have lost great swaths of land to them. And those damn cows eat up all the grass so the mustangs and other animals have nothing," Raina said. "I'm headed out for some air. You keep him company, but don't get him too excited, you hear?"

Lenora blushed and nodded. Once the heavy, industrial door swung closed, they were alone. Clay took her hand and brought it up to his lips.

"Are you okay?" He said.

"Oh, yes. I'm so happy you're alive," Lenora said. "I mean that. I was so scared yesterday."

"You were?" Clay said. "That's good."

"So, you're not coming back to the ranch to heal?"

"No, my Mom wants the chance to take care of me for a while. I think it's best anyway."

"Okay, I'll... I'll miss you," Lenora said.

"Oh yeah? How much?" Clay said. He was smiling and when she turned to look at him he pulled her down and kissed her swiftly. Then he groaned and lay still with his eyes closed.

"Oh, I'm sorry. Are you alright?" Lenora said. "Oh, no. That's my fault."

"I'm fine. Don't be sorry," Clay said. "I'm the one who moved. It's still so hard to breathe. And moving is sheer hell."

She touched his cheek and then wiped away the beads of sweat that appeared on his forehead. His skin was pale again, and the dark circles under his eyes stood out in stark contrast.

"I'm sorry, Clay," she said. "For the past. Can we go out for a ride when you come back? And talk?"

"What, are you worried I won't be able to give you the best night of your life anymore? I fell off a horse, I'm not dead!" Clay said.

"Actually, the horse fell on you. And you can joke about it, but you almost died yesterday and so, yes, we are all worried about you, and I want to tell you I'm sorry for making such a big deal over Crystal," Lenora said. "Now, can we just have a nice heart to heart talk when you get back, with no touching?"

"No touching ?" Clay said.

"Yes," Lenora said. "I mean I can't think straight with you touching me. So, if we ride separate horses, I'll be able to say what's on my mind."

"You can't think when I touch you?" Clay said. "Why did you hide this very important fact from me until now?" He ran his free hand across her thigh and then grasped her opposite hip and moved his thumb until it was under the fabric of her shirt and touching her bare side. "Let me make love to you right now."

"Clay, are you crazy?" Lenora said. "No!"

He smiled. "Aww, come on. I nearly died yesterday. You said so yourself. Why can't I want you here and now, in this

174

hospital bed?"

"I can't believe I'm even having this conversation." But she bent her head and touched her lips to his.

"I'll miss you, too," Clay said, and his eyes told her he meant every word.

***

Spring turned the ranch to green emerald pastures. Swallows built nests in the barns, and the fish spawned in the river. More guests than the ranch could accommodate tried to book a retreat at Bear Dance Ranch. Lenora found herself busy from the moment she woke until her head hit the pillow at night. Corbin was a good hand around the ranch. He took over Clay's string of training horses, and helped out with all the ranch work as well.

Lenora missed Clay. His absence was a steady ache located deep below her ribs. Some mornings when she woke, she could almost smell his scent on her pillow. She wanted nothing more than to roll over and be engulfed in his strong arms and rest her head on his chest. Cell service was spotty at the reservation. The few times she was able to speak to him Clay sounded happy and as if he was having a great time catching up with old friends. His mother was pampering him through recovery.

Nearly a year to the day of Lenora's arrival at Bear Dance Ranch, Clay came home.

High atop the middle foothill to the east, Lenora saw the old Ford Raina drove kicking up a dust plume. She urged Major into a full gallop, and the two of them raced across the brilliant green pastures, cattle scattering to get out of their way. In the driveway in front of the ranch house, a group had formed around Clay and his mother. Slipping off her blowing horse, Lenora stood and watched as Clay hugged her aunt and uncle for a good three minutes. Annie was crying when they finally pulled apart, and so Clay hugged her again.

"There you are," Clay said. "I thought that was you

tearing down out of the hills. No one else on this ranch would ride a crazy, white Arabian." He locked eyes with Lenora, and she was reminded of their first introduction on a similar evening a year ago. How much had changed, she thought. She had never imagined this cowboy would come to mean so much to her.

"Welcome home, Clay," Lenora said. She hoped her face showed all the pleasure she felt to see him standing before her, nearly healed and so strong. Her face was starting to flush. He was giving her the look which seemed to mean he knew what color her panties wore— or at least he would like to find out.

"Come inside for dinner," Annie said. "Lenora has made lasagna, and there is fresh bread."

Lenora put Major away, then headed into the ranch house. The table was alive with stories of the ranch and all that had happened in Clay's absence. Jesse and Corbin explained all about the training horses and what had been accomplished with each animal.

"No riding colts, Clay," Annie said. "Until the doctor releases you."

"That is for darn sure," Raina said.

Lenora caught Clay watching her several times, and each time he winked. Would she be able to sneak out to see him later? His mother might be staying in his bunkhouse. Plus with Corbin out there, too, it seemed highly unlikely. Maybe, she thought, she could take him out on a leisurely trail ride tomorrow for some much needed privacy.

"Clay, Annie and I have been talking," Byron said. "And we'd like Corbin to stay on if he wants to. After speaking with your momma, Corbin, she tells us you've hung up your spurs and bucking saddle and aren't doing the rodeo anymore, so maybe it's time you found yourself a good ranch to be part of. You think about it. With so many guests coming to the ranch now, and well, Lenora wants to expand even more. I know Clay is going to need to start back slow as well, so there will be some slack to fill around this place."

"Yes sir, I'd like that pretty well," Corbin said.

"Me, too," Clay said. "Someone has to keep an eye on you and all those ladies you like to bring home."

"To Clay coming back to Bear Dance," Annie said. "And to Corbin staying on."

Everyone raised their glasses and Lenora felt herself smiling so much her cheeks began to ache.

EPILOGUE

The moon was full. Lenora undressed and stood in her panties and white tank top, looking out the window at the clear sky filled with the silver rays from the moon. She watched as Clay emerged from the barn, and she wondered what he was doing out so late at night. He looked up at her window and waved to her before disappearing into the barn. A few moments later, he reappeared with Moon, his big, gentle mare. Clay led the horse right up to her window and motioned for her to open it. Pulling a cardigan around her shoulders, she did so.

"Come down, please," Clay said. His eyes were so dark and sad and sweet.

She was reminded of the first time they went night riding last spring. The air carried the hint of growing things to come, and the stars shone with a softer brilliance than they had in the winter months. So much had changed over the course of a year, and yet, again, she found her heart beating with such excitement, she swore it would wake her sleeping aunt and uncle. As she slipped down the heavy staircase, avoiding the squeaky treads, she had to remind herself to breathe. When she stepped out on the porch, he had the mare positioned so she could use the steps to mount bareback. Once on, she felt Clay swing up behind her and his strong arms surrounded her. He smelled of oiled leather and mint. She could not help but sigh and relax into his grip; her nerve endings tingling with pleasure to be so close to him again.

The pines threw long shadows in the moonlight, and the night was so still, the only sounds were the mare's hooves in the dark. The faintest hint of wood smoke from the ranch house teased Lenora's nose, but otherwise they could have been thousands of miles from any other human beings. Moon's ears swiveled, and she blew gently, she seemed as happy as Lenora to have Clay back.

Neither Lenora nor Clay spoke a word. Lenora was too caught up in the beauty of the night and the amazing feeling of being, once again, in the arms of the man she loved most in this world. They left the barns and dark houses and made their way into the moonlight. Halfway up the trail she felt his mouth against her ear, and he began to whisper.

"I've missed you so much these past months. I kept remembering the way you looked when you first showed up here with your horse and scared half to death. You were so determined to do everything yourself, but you started letting me in very slowly. And then you let me make love to you after that rain storm, and I knew you were the only woman in the world for me."

He paused, and she could tell he was looking out over the expanse of valley below them. Her own heart was beating so fast she wondered if he could feel it even through all their clothes. She wanted to say something, but she was too afraid he did not mean what she thought he meant. She let him gather his thoughts and finish.

"Lenora, what I'm trying to say is," he paused to brush his hand across her cheek. "Please give me another chance. You're all I want. You're so much more than I deserve."

He stopped the mare and slid down but kept his hands around her waist. He held her gently. With the brightness of the moon, she could see his eyes clearly.

"And I love you so much that sometimes I can barely breathe when I think about not having you in my life."

A surge of pure happiness, as rich and alive as the star-laced sky overhead, surged through Lenora's heart. She pulled off her glove and brushed her fingers across Clay's cheek.

"We are perfect together. I won't hurt you, I promise. You're safe with me. Lenora, I want you to be mine. Please?"

He glanced down and then back up, and his eyes were bright and glittery with the diamonds of unshed tears. She felt light headed. She slipped off the mare into his arms. To be with this man, to be his and he to be hers, she knew she wanted this with her whole being.

"Say something, Nora?" Clay sounded desperate. "Please? Tell me what's in your heart? I swear I can't tell sometimes."

He wiped the tears from her cheeks, which she had not even noticed were falling. Smiling and then laughing, she realized only then that her lips were sealed.

"My heart is so full, Clay. It feels like all the stars in the sky are exploding inside me right now." She took a deep breathe. He was smiling at her, his eyes soft in the pale light from the moon.

"I love you, too," she whispered.

He bent his head and kissed her, and the very ground seemed to shift beneath her feet. Thankfully, with Clay's arms to steady her, she no longer worried about falling.

ABOUT THE AUTHOR

Christina Rhoads resides on an Arabian horse farm where she divides her time (when she isn't fixing fence or stacking hay) between writing novels, painting and training equines. While studying creative writing as she earned a BA in English from Indiana University, she fell madly in love with the act of creating characters and then sharing them with the world.

She often describes her ideal afternoon as one spent riding her horse, Major Temptation, and then curling up with a good book and cup of peppermint tea.

For more on Christina's books check out her website or connect with her on social media.

www.christinarhoads.com

https://www.facebook.com/Christina-Rhoads-212417315991236/

https://www.instagram.com/christina.rhoads.author/?hl=en